ROBERT
STIKMANZ

STIKMANTICA
AUSTIN, TEXAS

This is a work of fiction. Names, characters, historical accounts and locales are fruits of the author's imagination. Any resemblance to actual places or events, or to real persons, living or dead, is entirely coincidental.

Cover art, book design & entire contents by Robert Stikmanz

ISBN: 978-1-7321187-0-6

STIKMANTICA
stikmantica.com

Foreword

The Song of Worlds ([illegible]), recounts in verse the origin of a people, a struggle they lost, and a new home made through art and resilience. The poem's seven chapters peer back through 197 stanzas to a bardic history gnarly with myth before the ancestors of these lines were dreamed.

Although the poem indisputably emerged among the Dvarsh and in their tongue, nowhere are they named in it. The community at the narrative's center is called "the children of hills" ([illegible]), and individuals alone or together are "spinners" ([illegible]). Those who know the Dvarsh will recognize these as words they commonly use to describe themselves. Always, the story has been regarded as theirs, but whether these labels were original to the poem or descend from a remoter past I do not know.

There is no tradition of single authorship behind *The Song* ([illegible]). No Dvarsh Homer chants through its cadences. Quite the contrary, the story of *The Song*, what ordinary Dvarsh say when they talk about it, speaks of different poets at different hearths mingling memories. Big trauma and big joy both take many tongues to process.

The story of *The Song* also claims an age passed as variations jostled for place and wore smooth enough to snug into a single account. That happened long ago. The form in which the poem survives is very old, unchanged for far longer than a single age. Until now.

Adapting the received text for a human audience involved challenges. The written Dvarsh of the oldest extant authoritative copy captures an odd moment in the development of early modern conventions. Imagine Shelley's poetry with *Beowulf's* punctuation. The Dvarsh have been writing for millennia—they claim, with straight faces, to have invented the whole business—but for them punctuation is a relatively new devil. Very conservative Dvarsh hardly use it at all. They account grudging dashes here and there as major concessions to a decline of standards, and mutter darkly about arrogant disambiguity and punctuationists.

I have tried to respect their sensibility because otherwise I would never hear the end of it. Nevertheless, I have added dashes when clarity wanted them. Quite a lot of dashes, actually. In a couple of places, I even added Dvarsh equivalents of question and quotation marks. Innovation went no further. Despite urging from Dvarsh avant-gardists to salt this presentation with their versions of commas and periods, I did not. Someone else can rush that barricade.

For material support, encouragement and dedicated friendship to this project and to me, I thank Rick Adams, Brent Caudle, Paul E. Cooley, Bonnie Cox, Carol Daeley, Patricia Daeley, Jim Eidson, Thomas Fang, David Gray, MJ Jirik, Kenneth Kidder, Glenn Lewis, Mark Lewis, William Luthans, Carla Maywald, Bram Meehan, James Rossignol, Nancy Salay, Kim Beauchemin Scoulios, and Erin Severe-Fudge. But for these stalwarts this book, if it existed at all, would be much reduced.

Robert Stikmanz

[illegible]

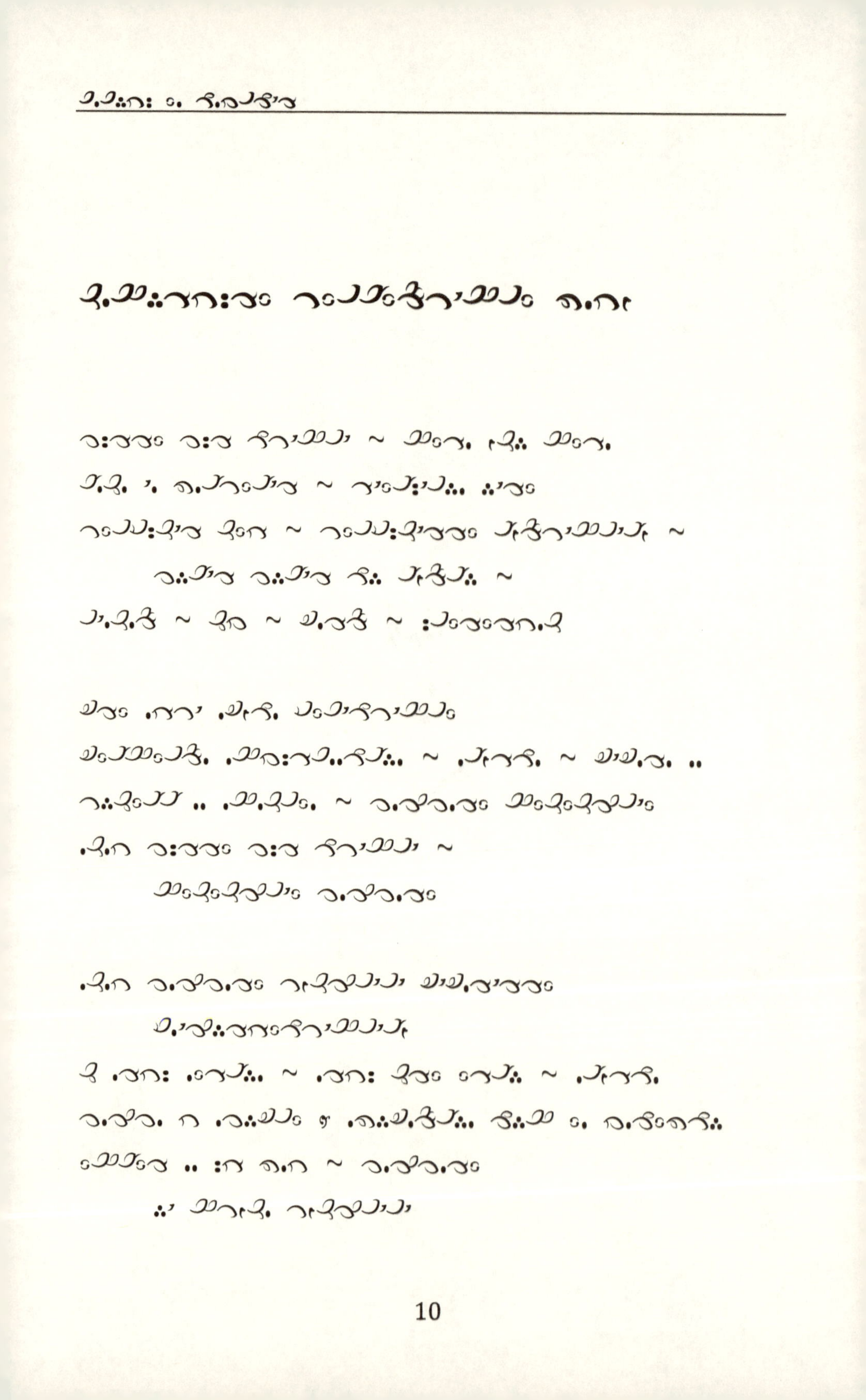

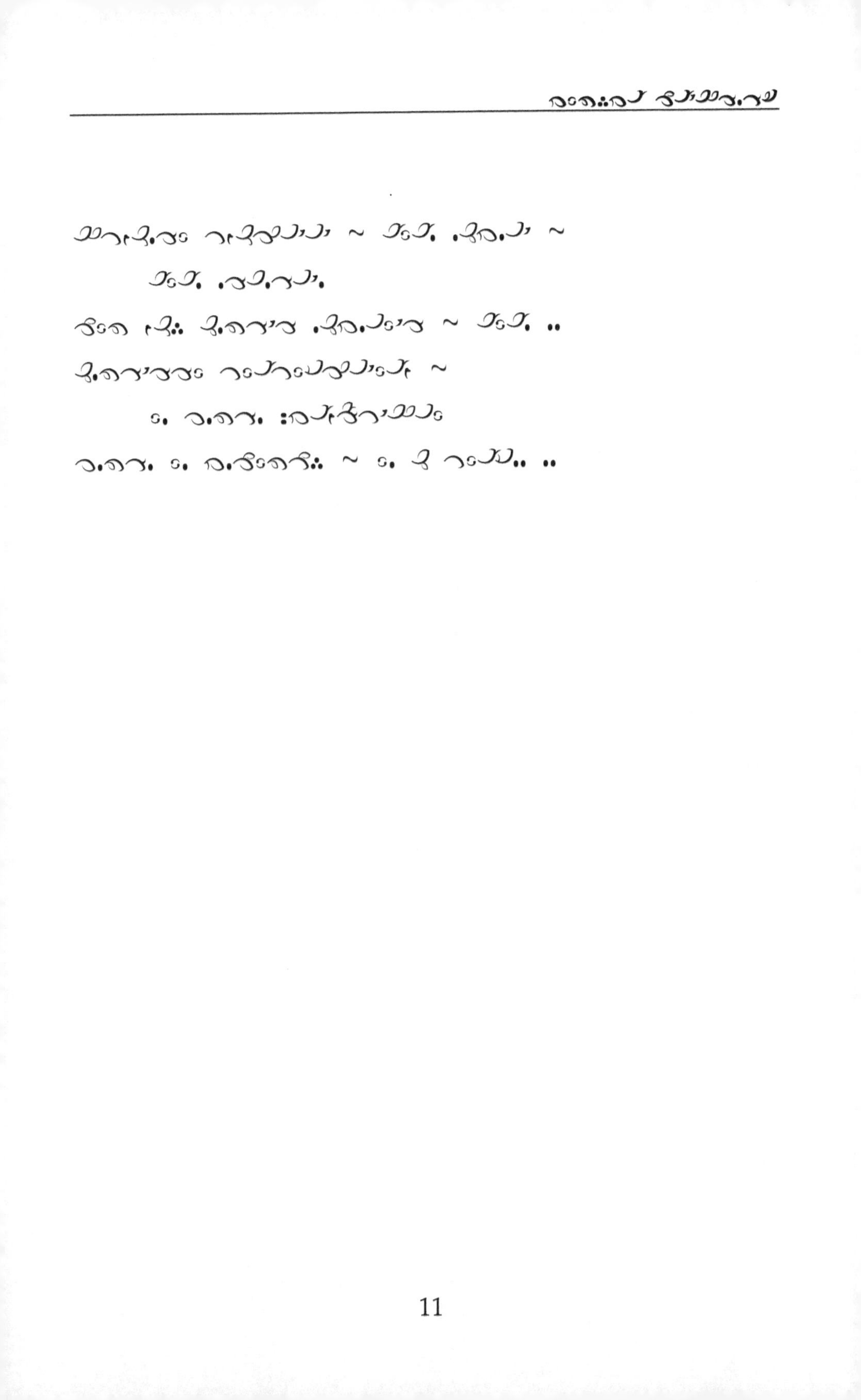

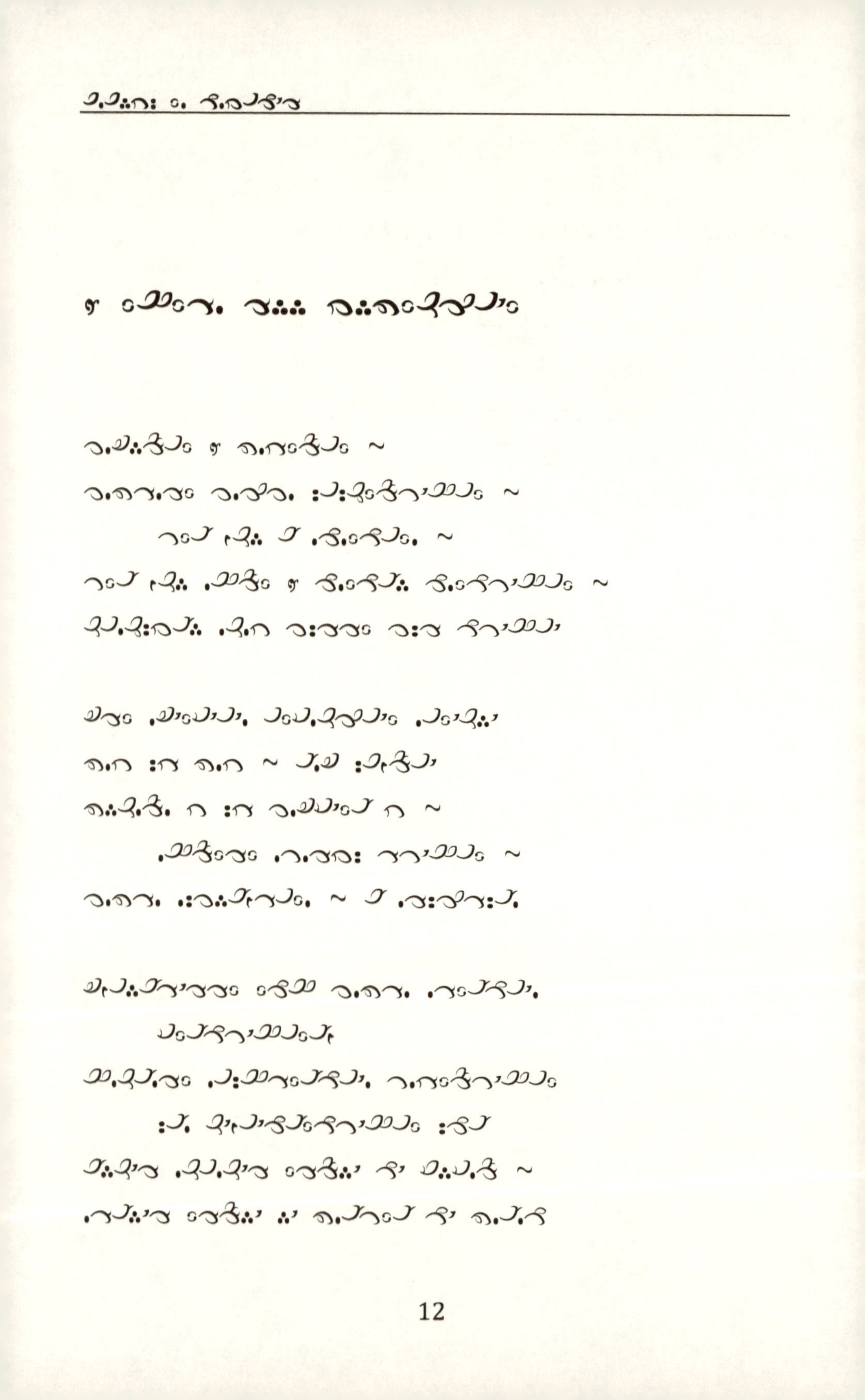

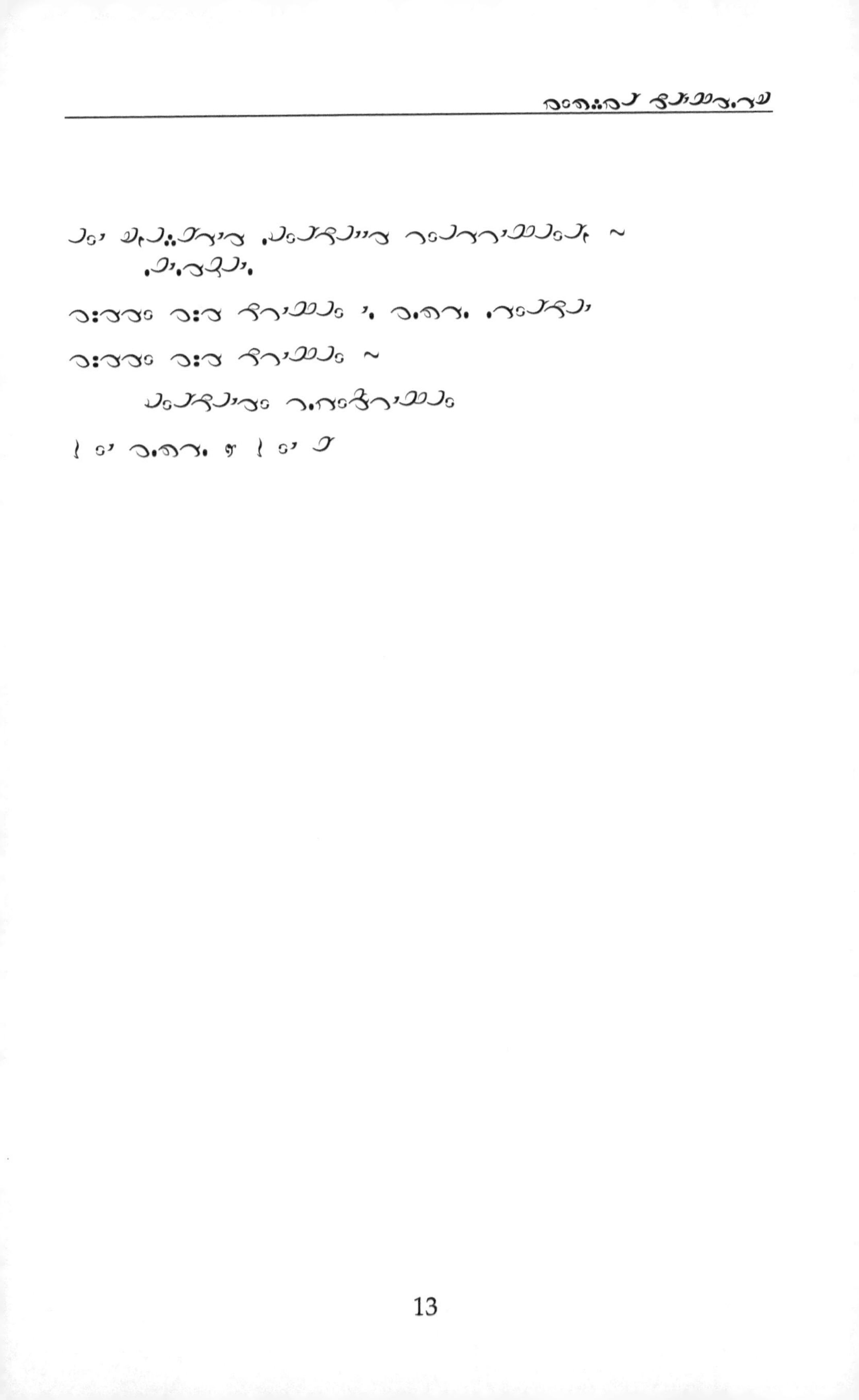

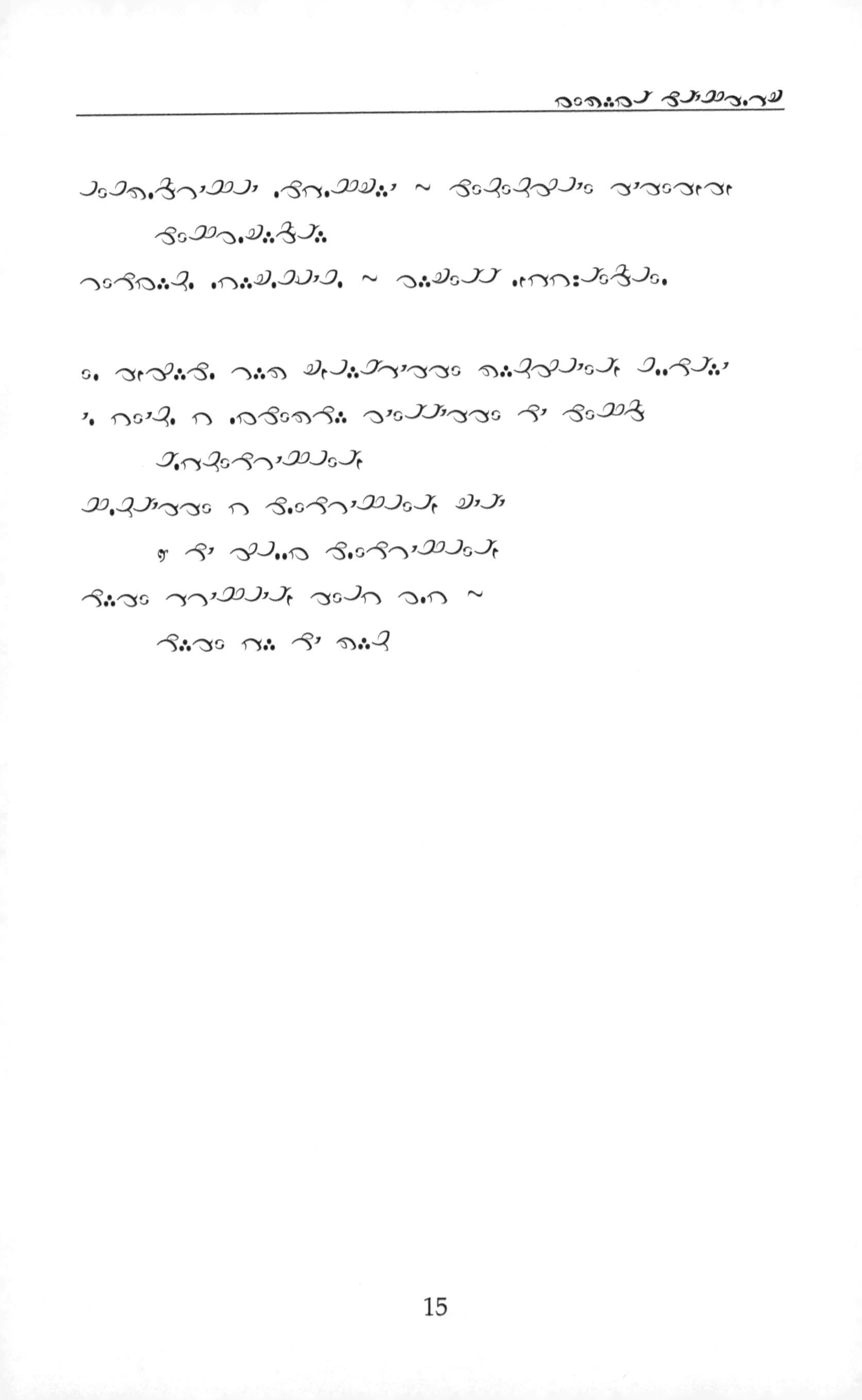

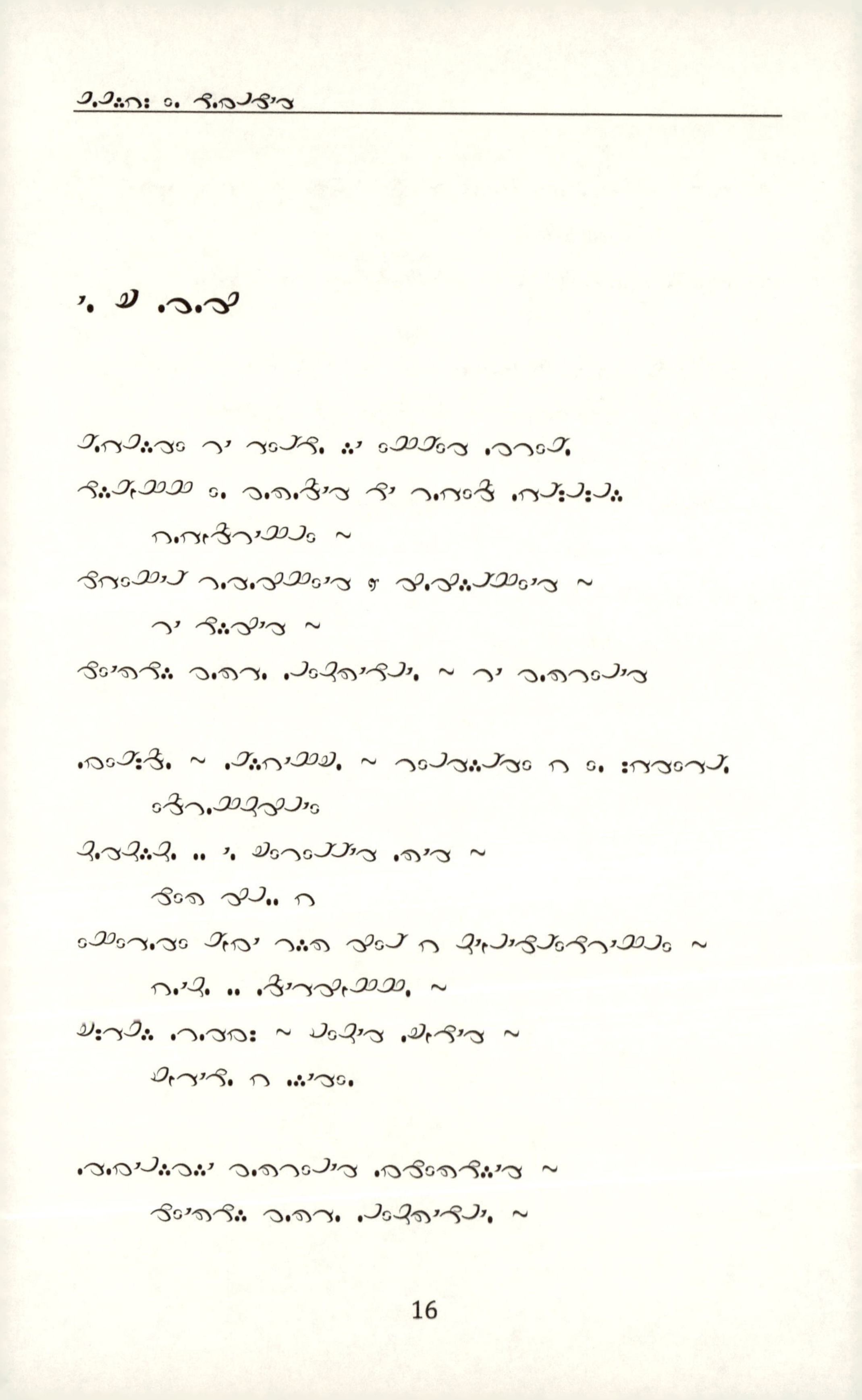

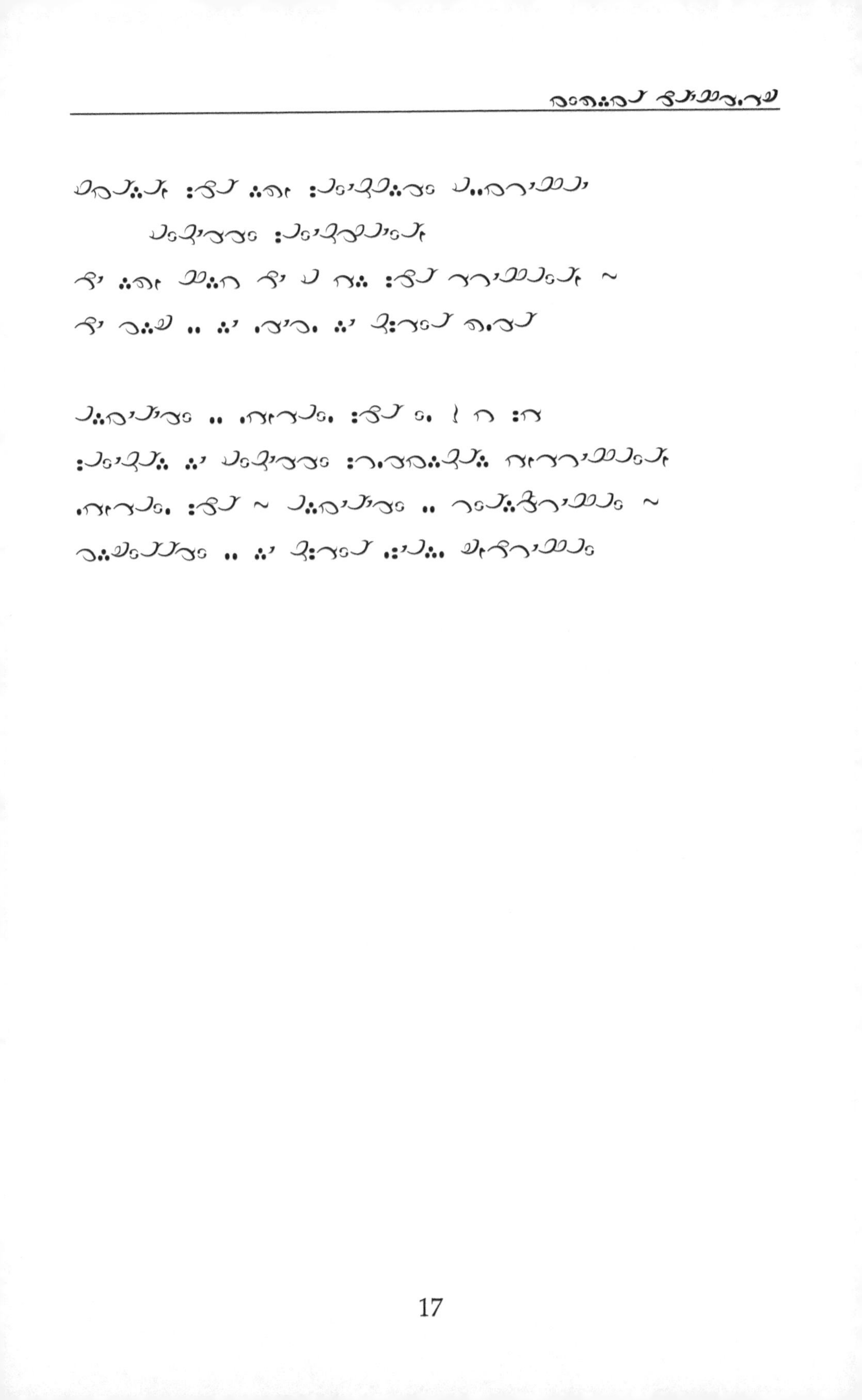

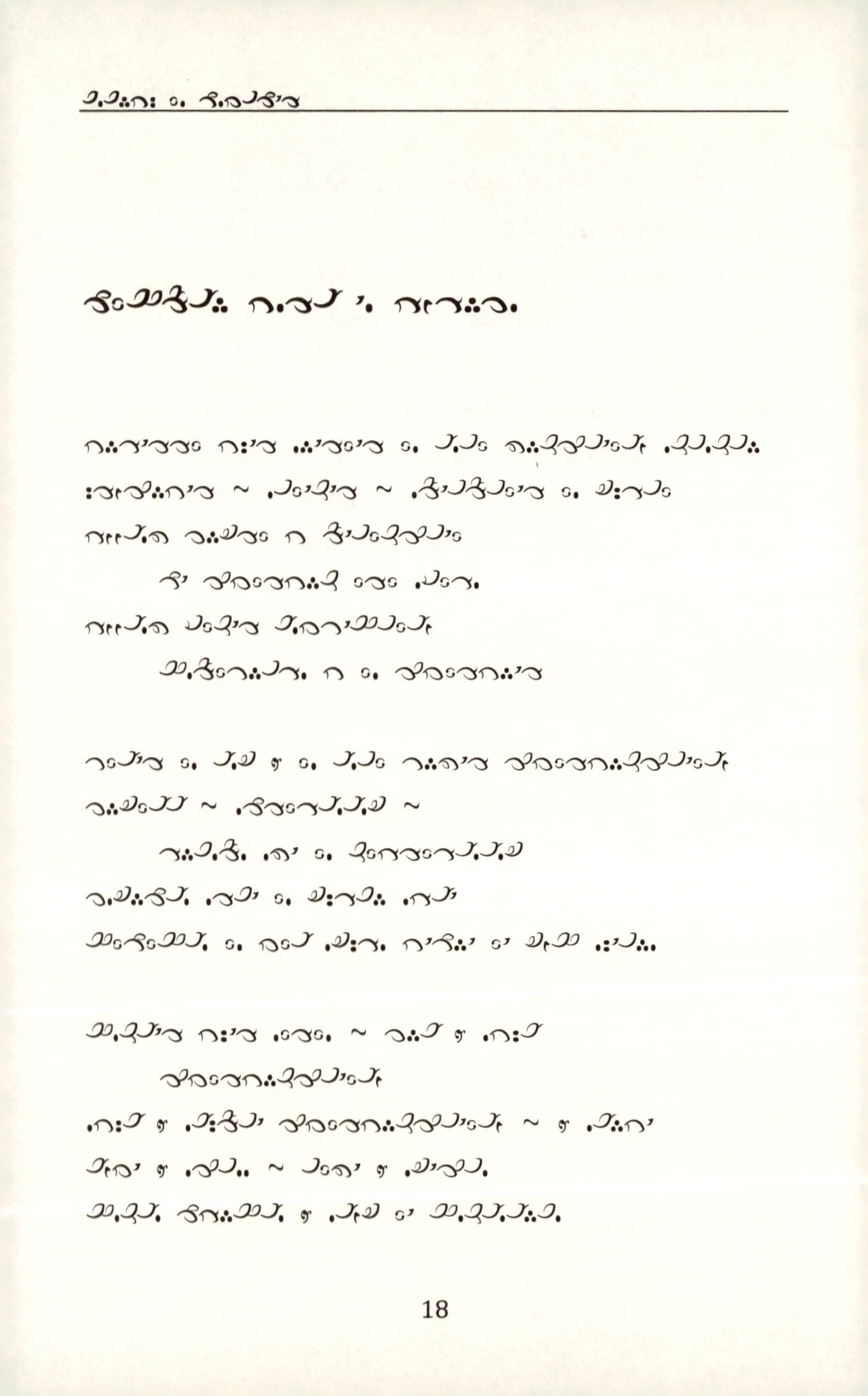

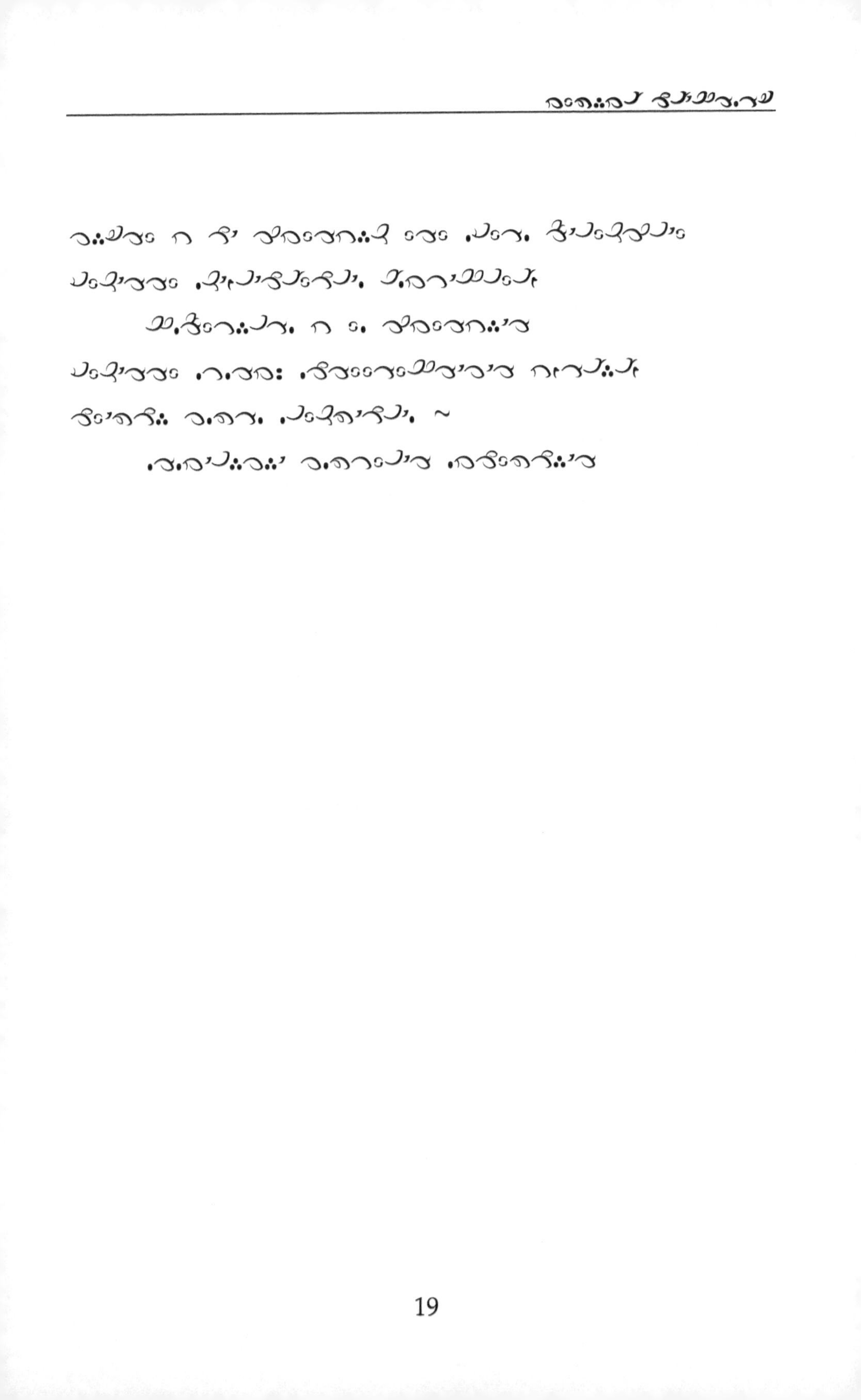

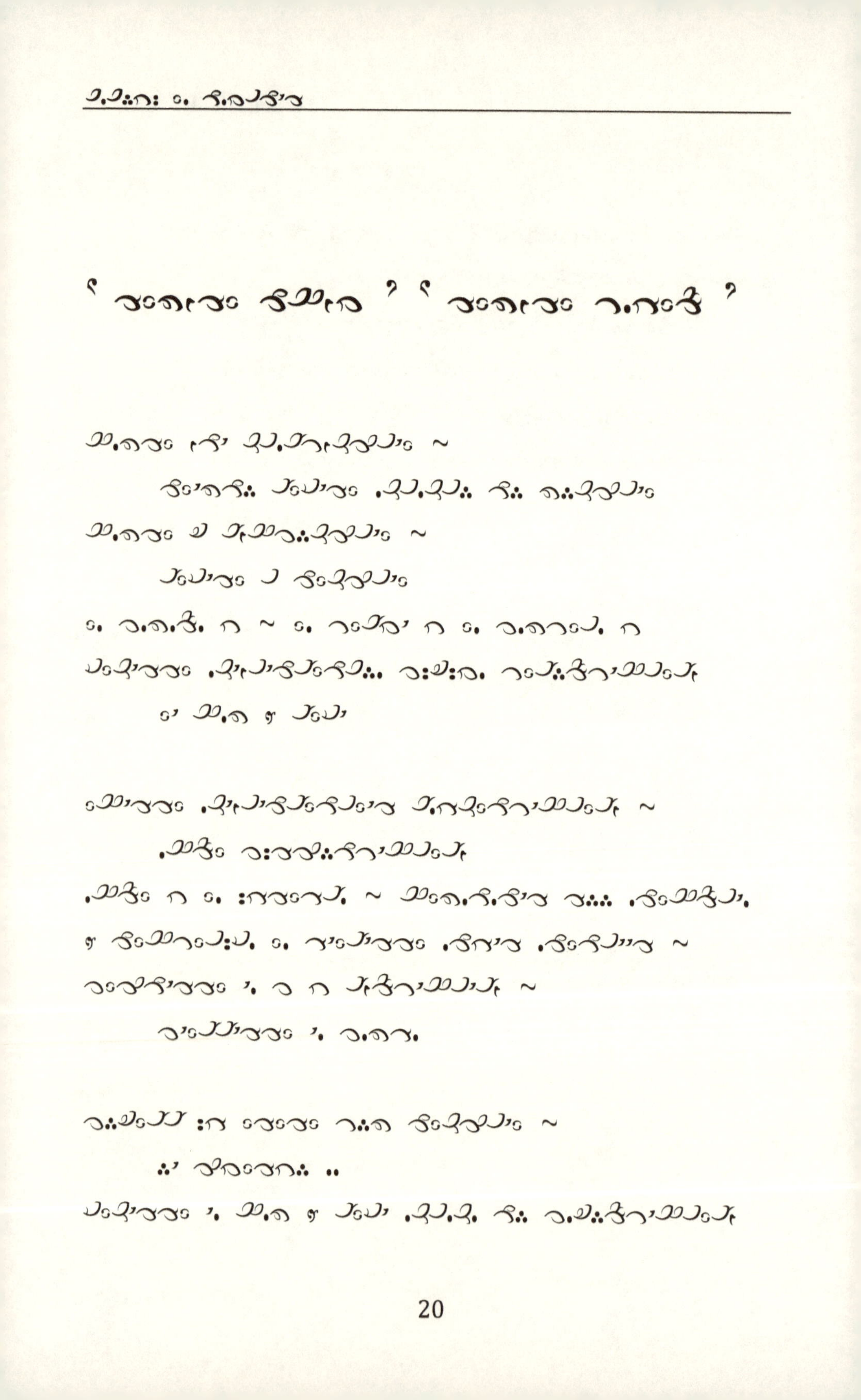

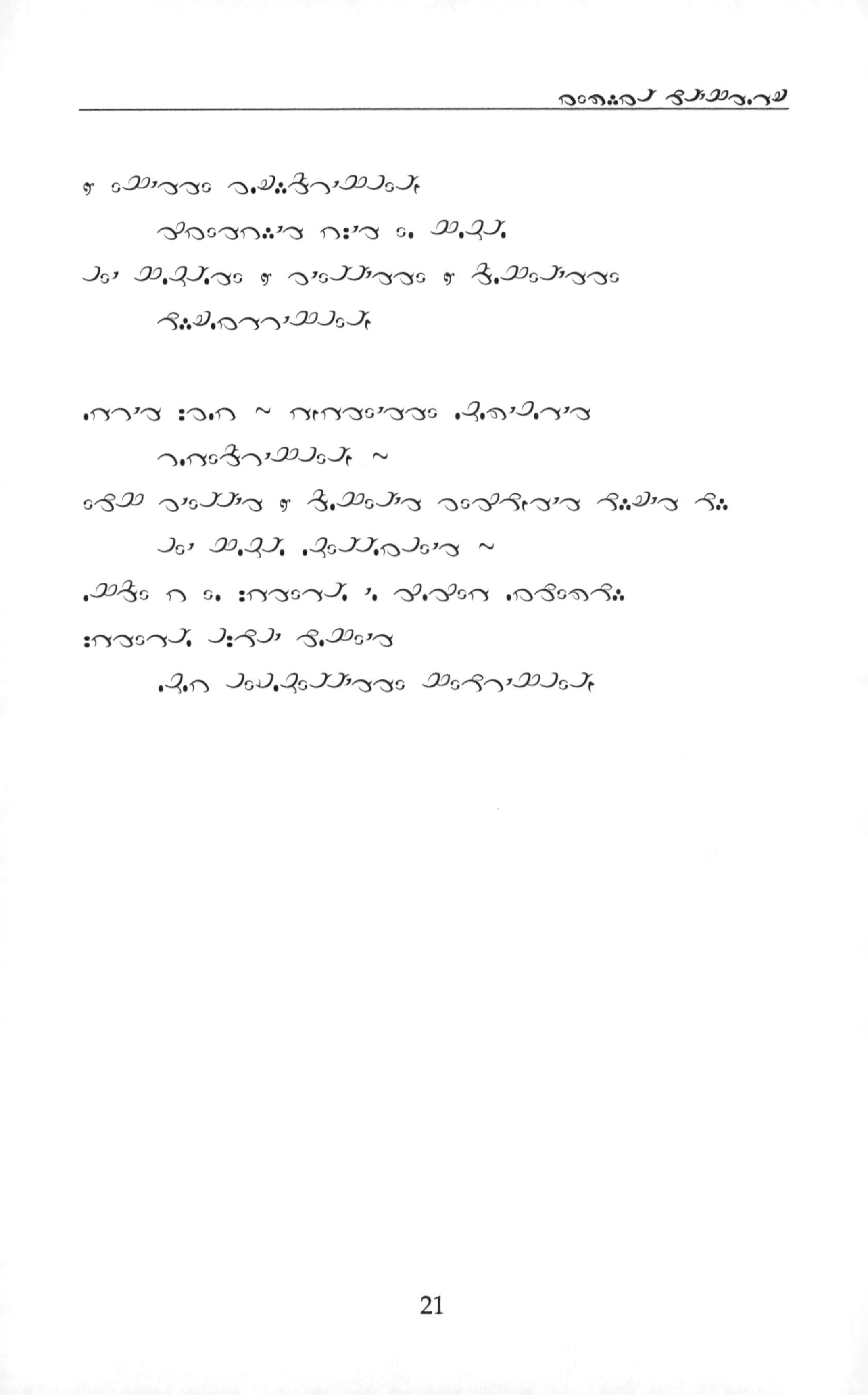

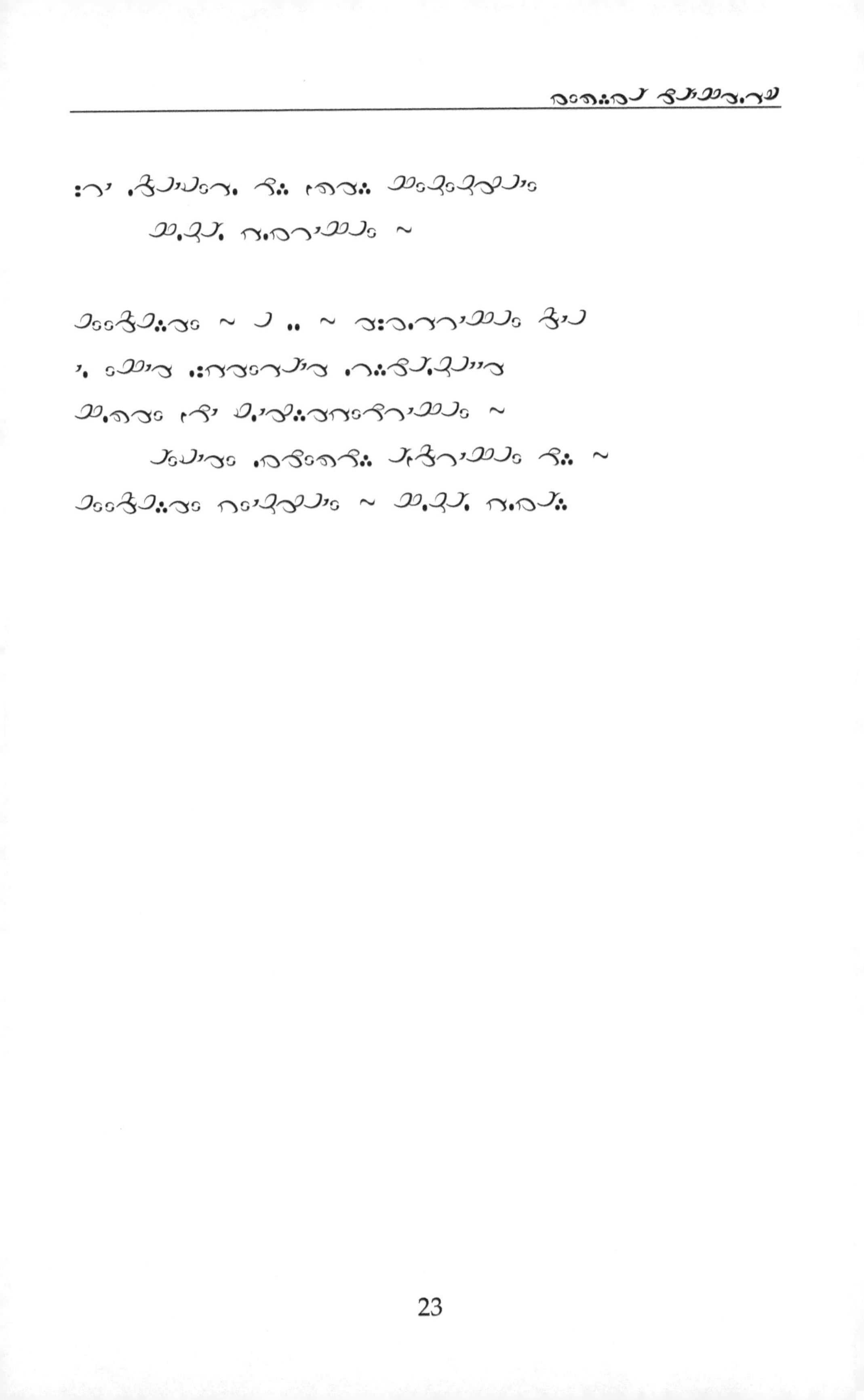

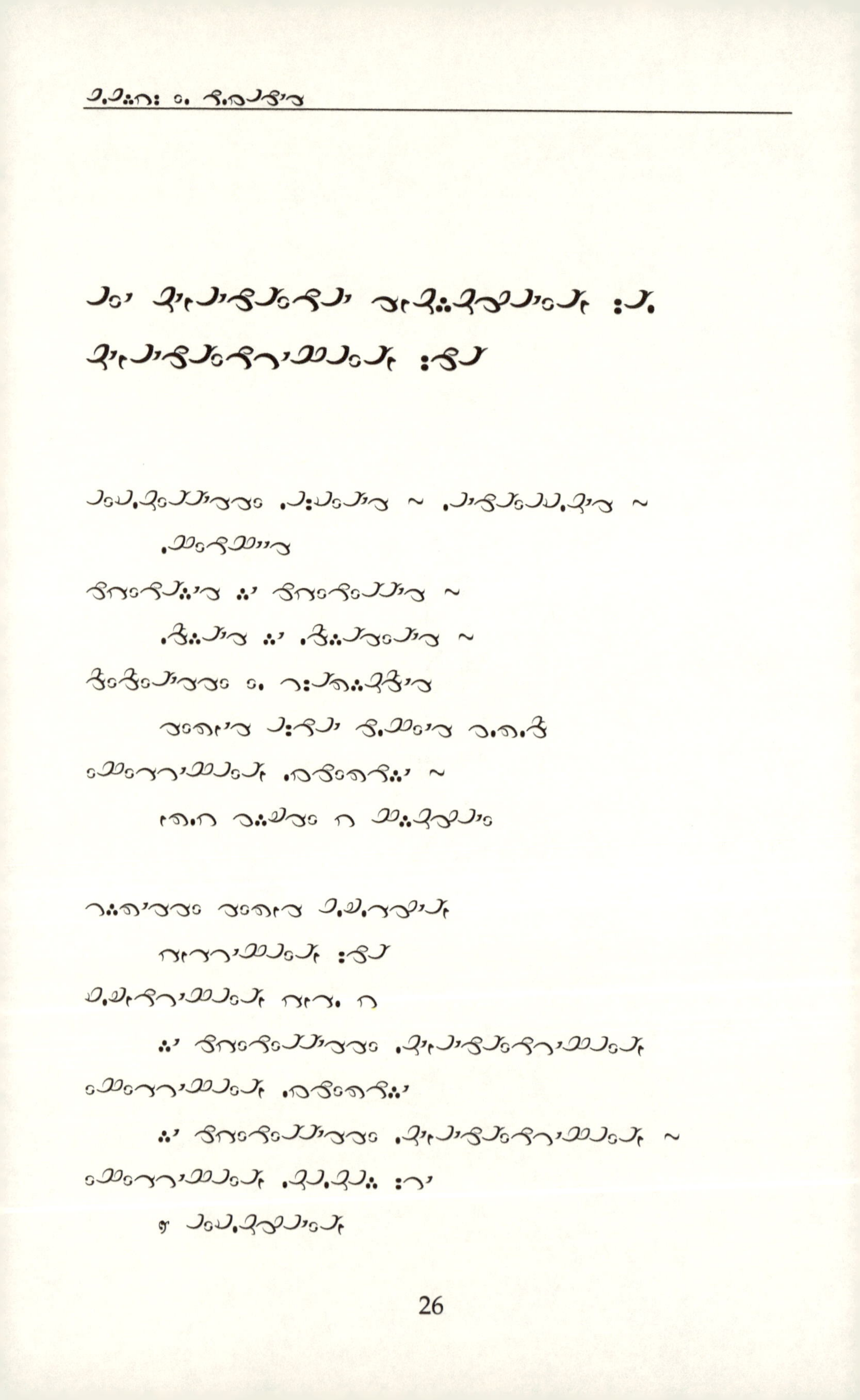

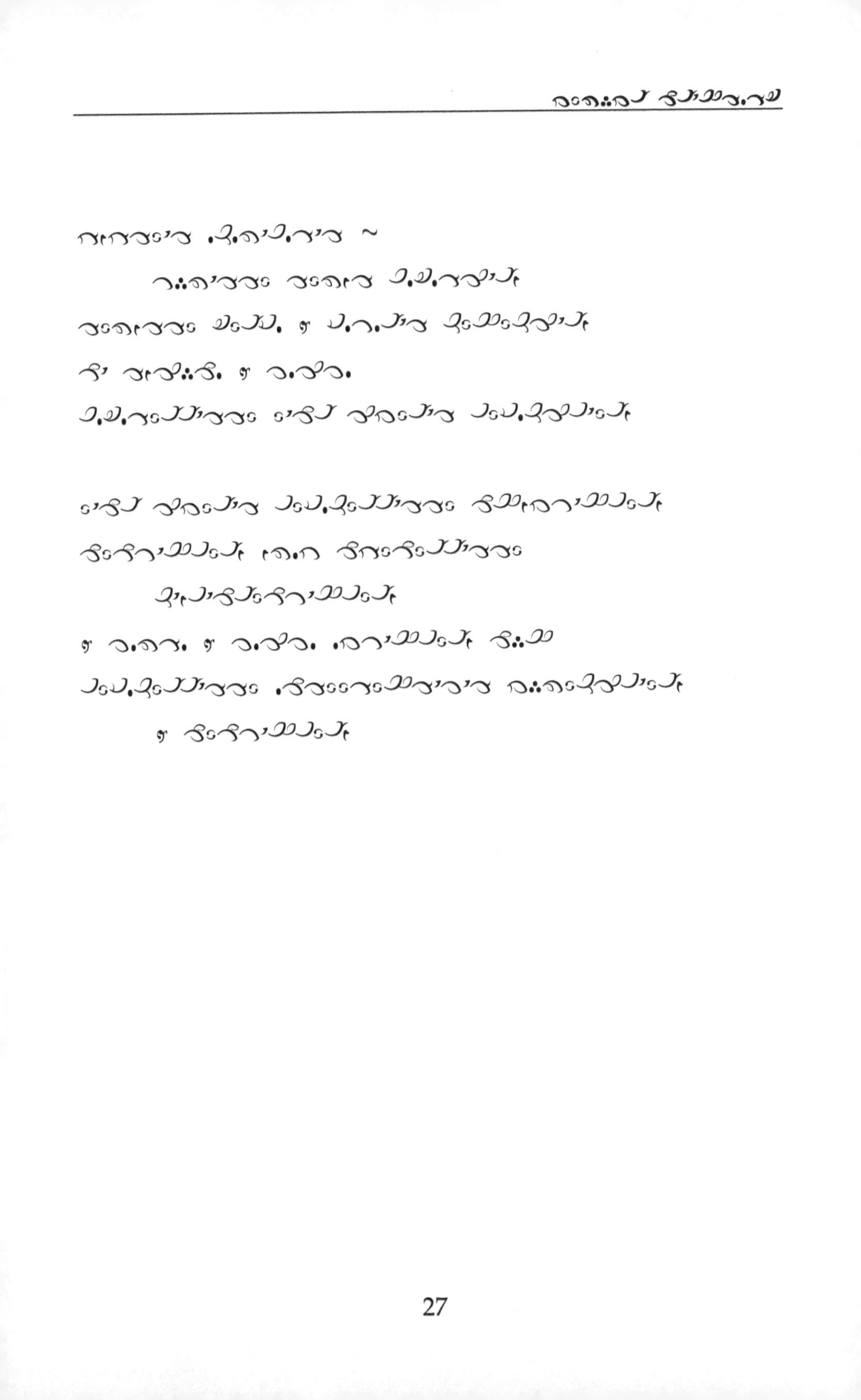

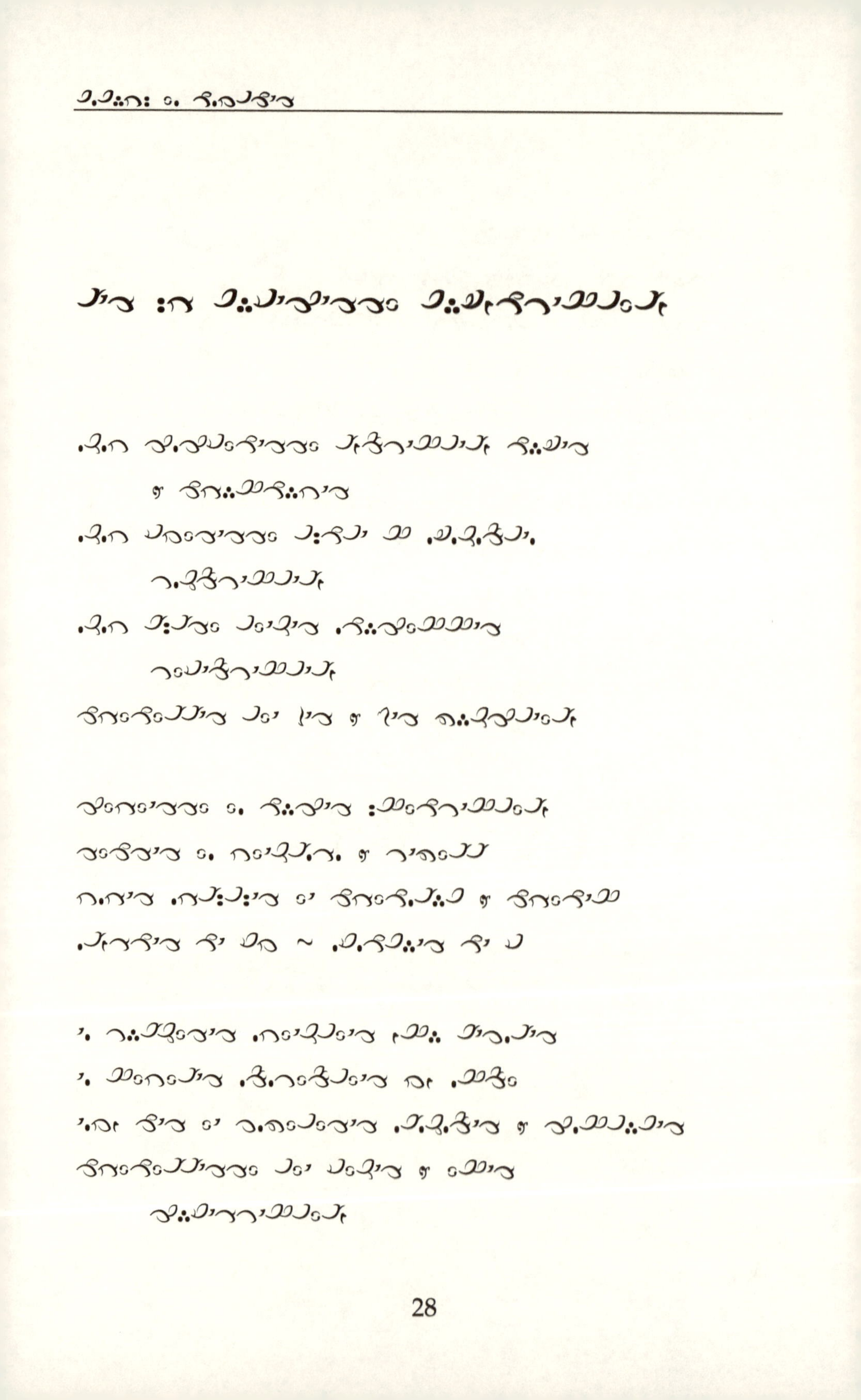

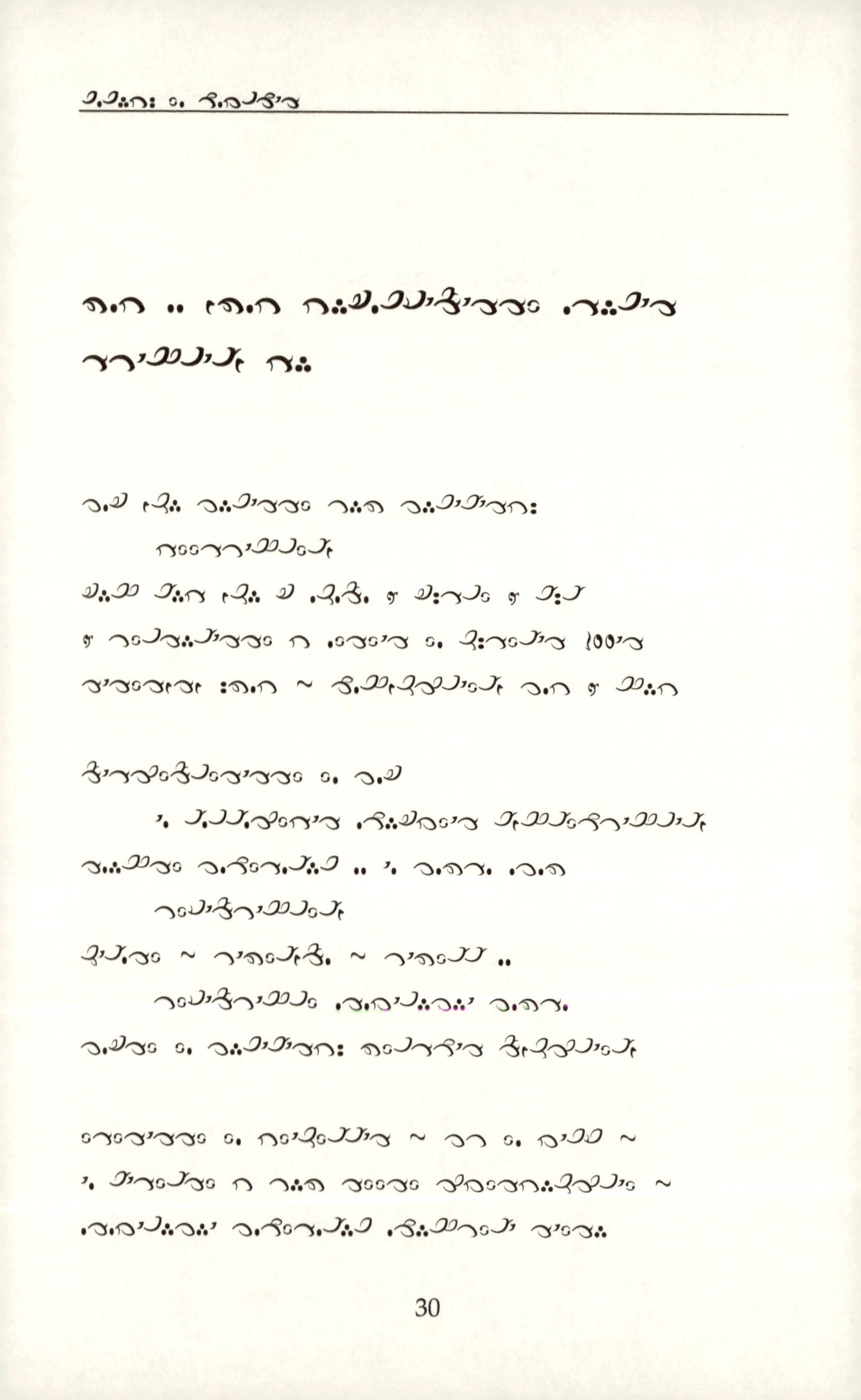

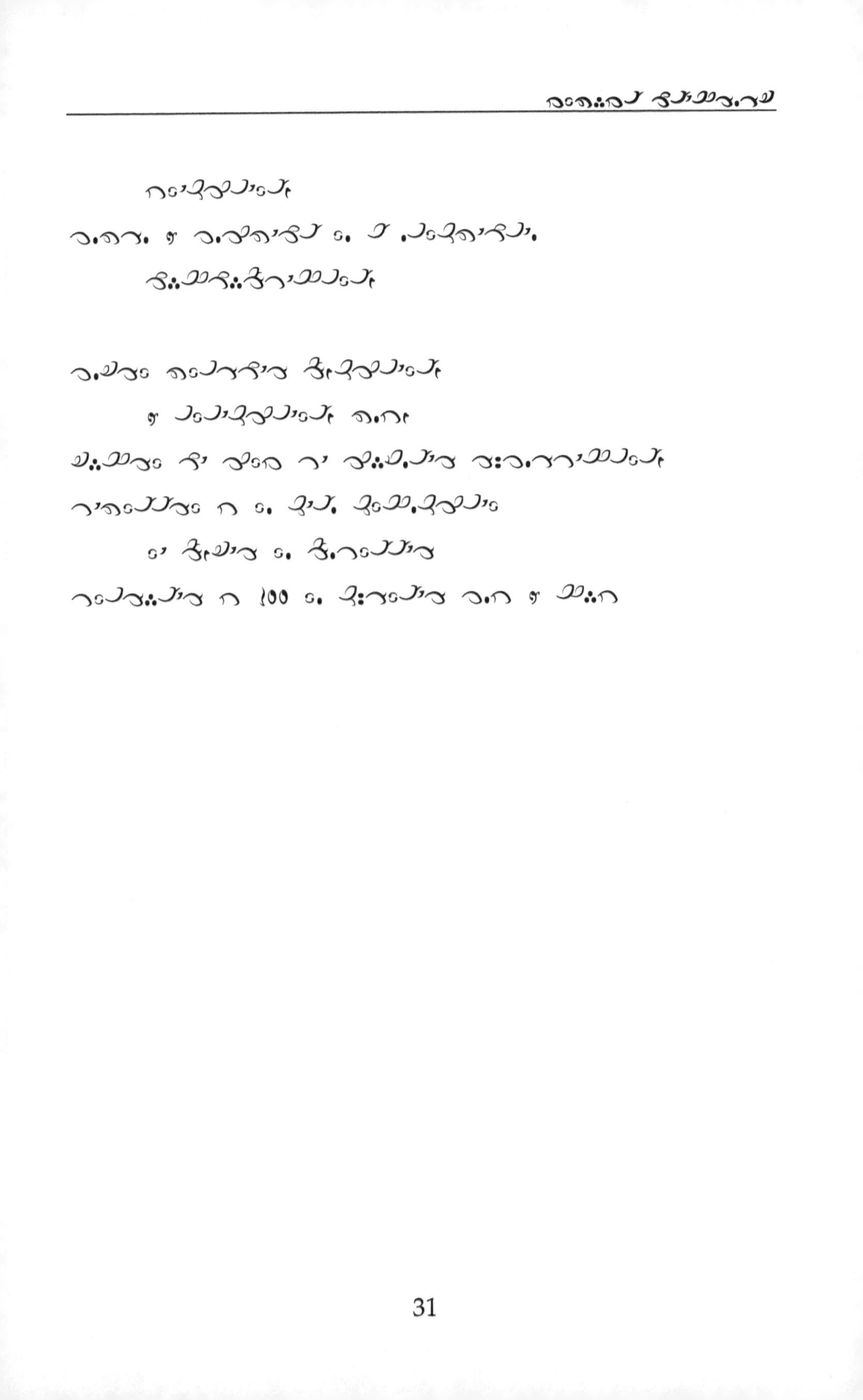

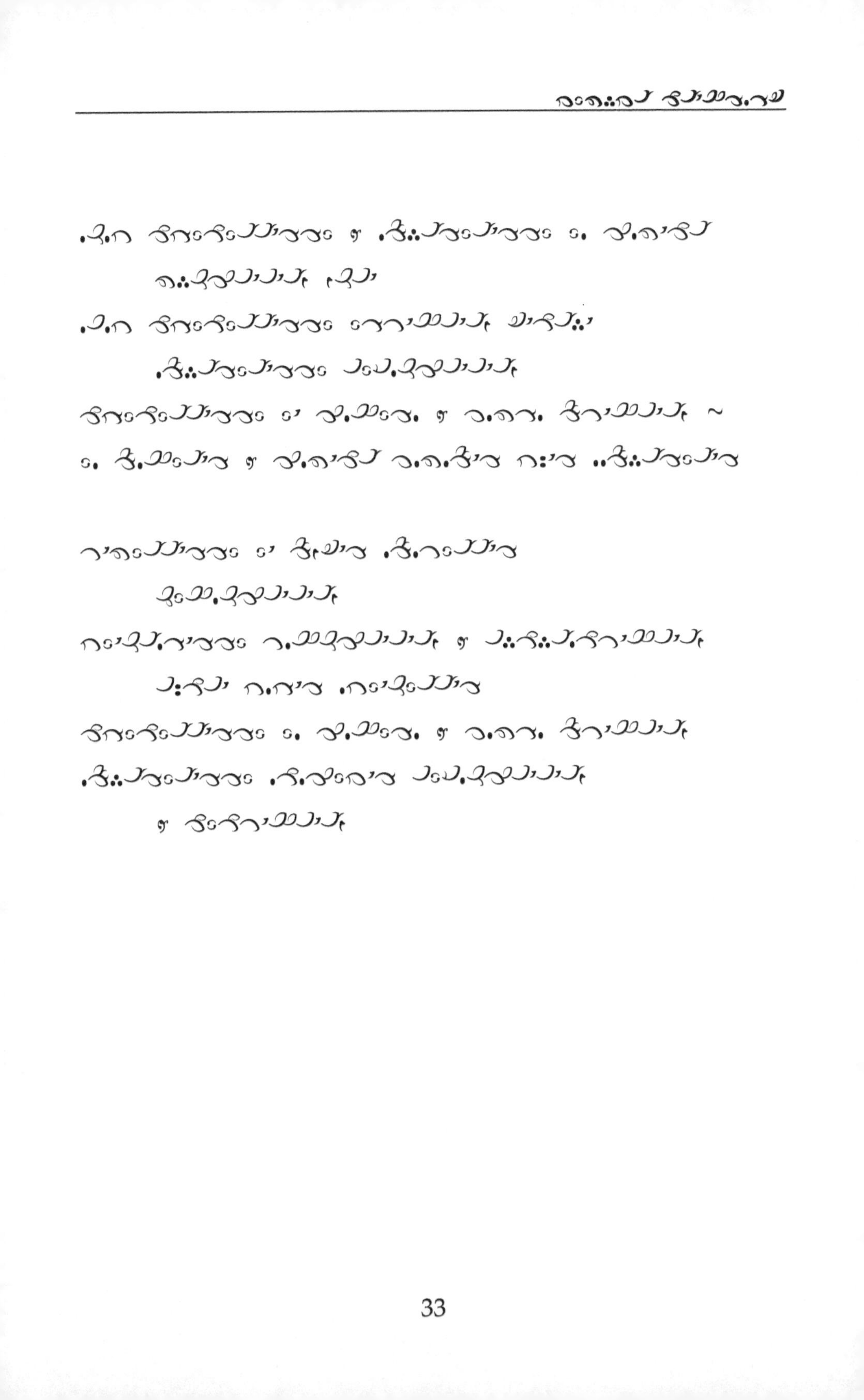

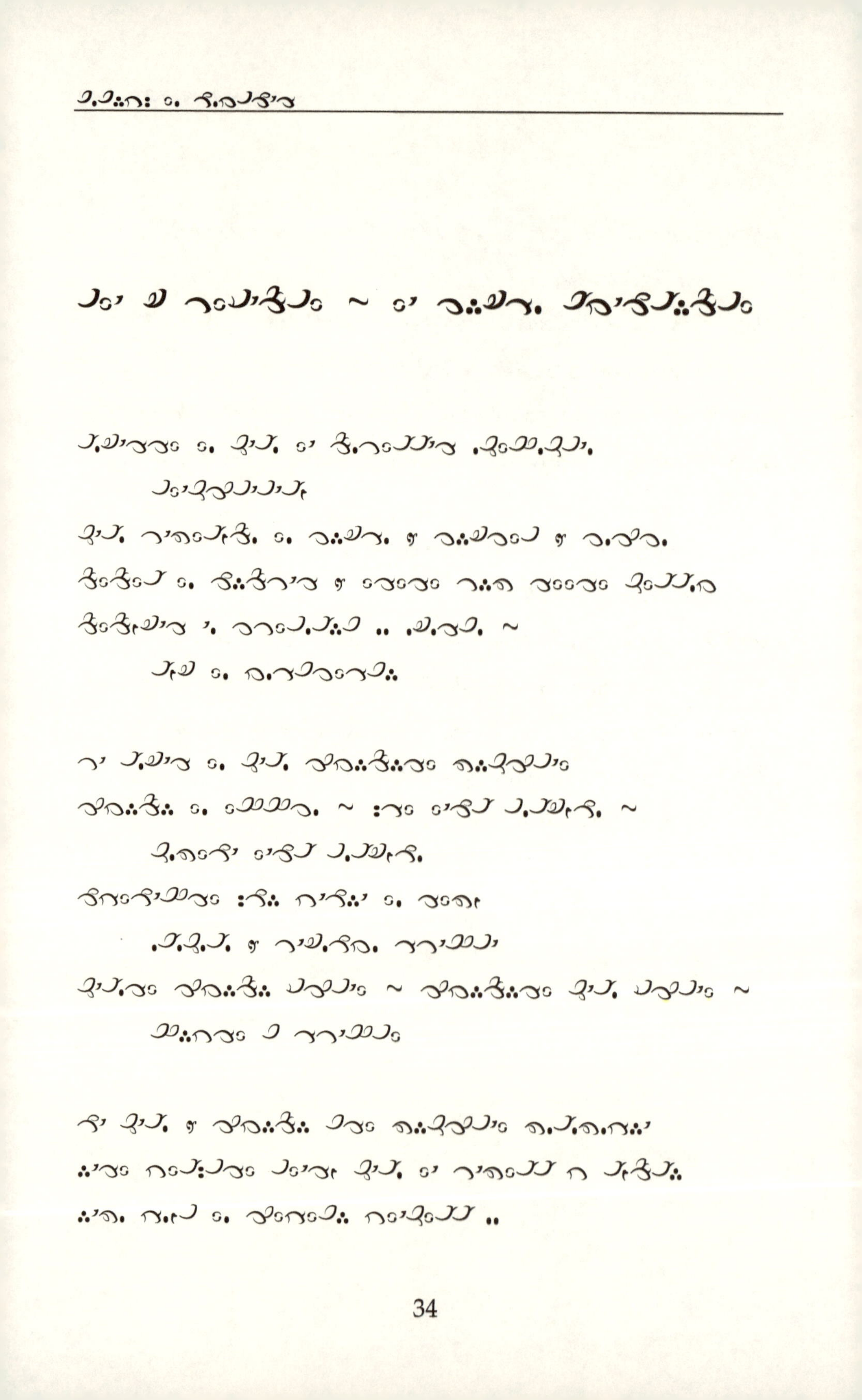

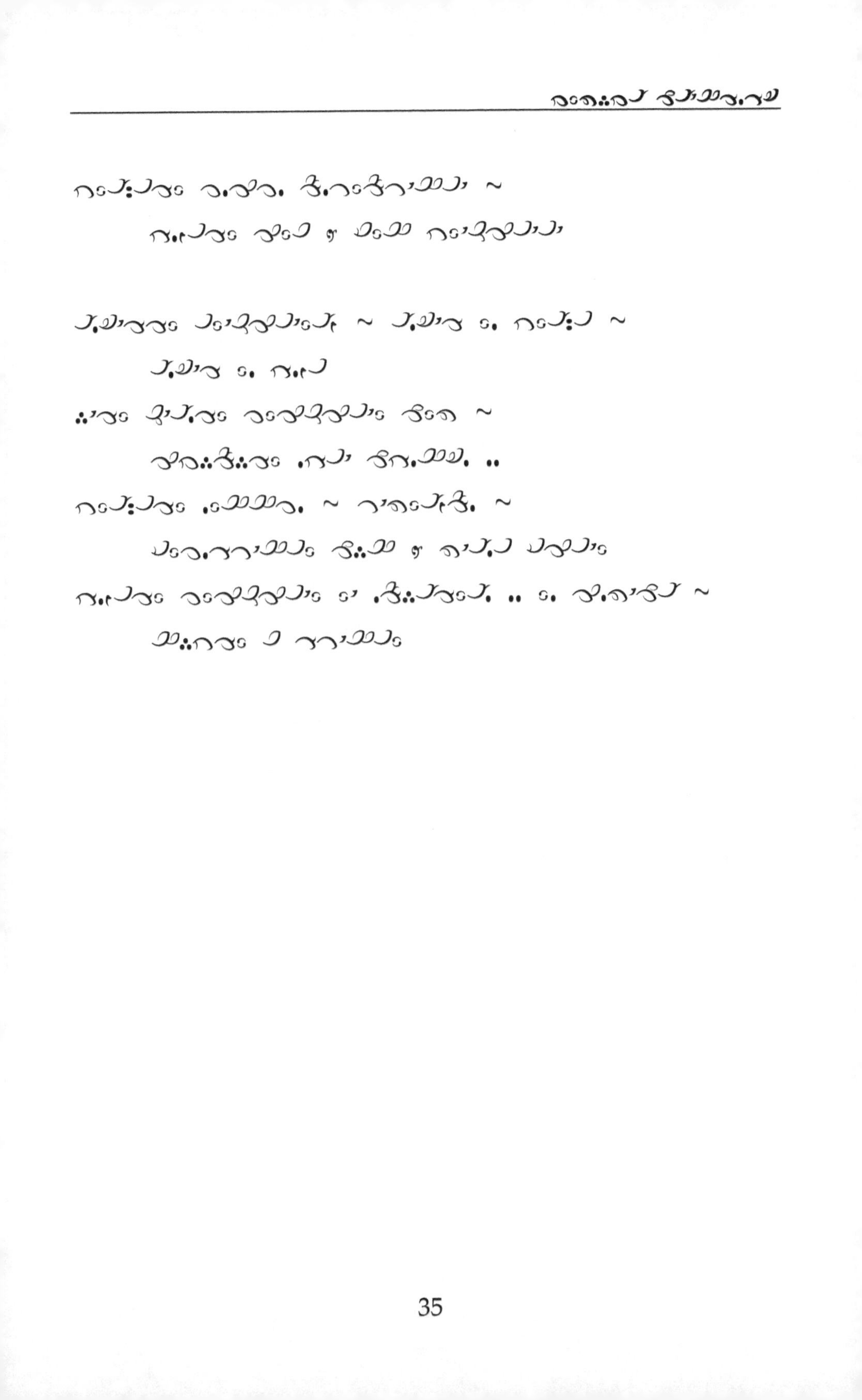

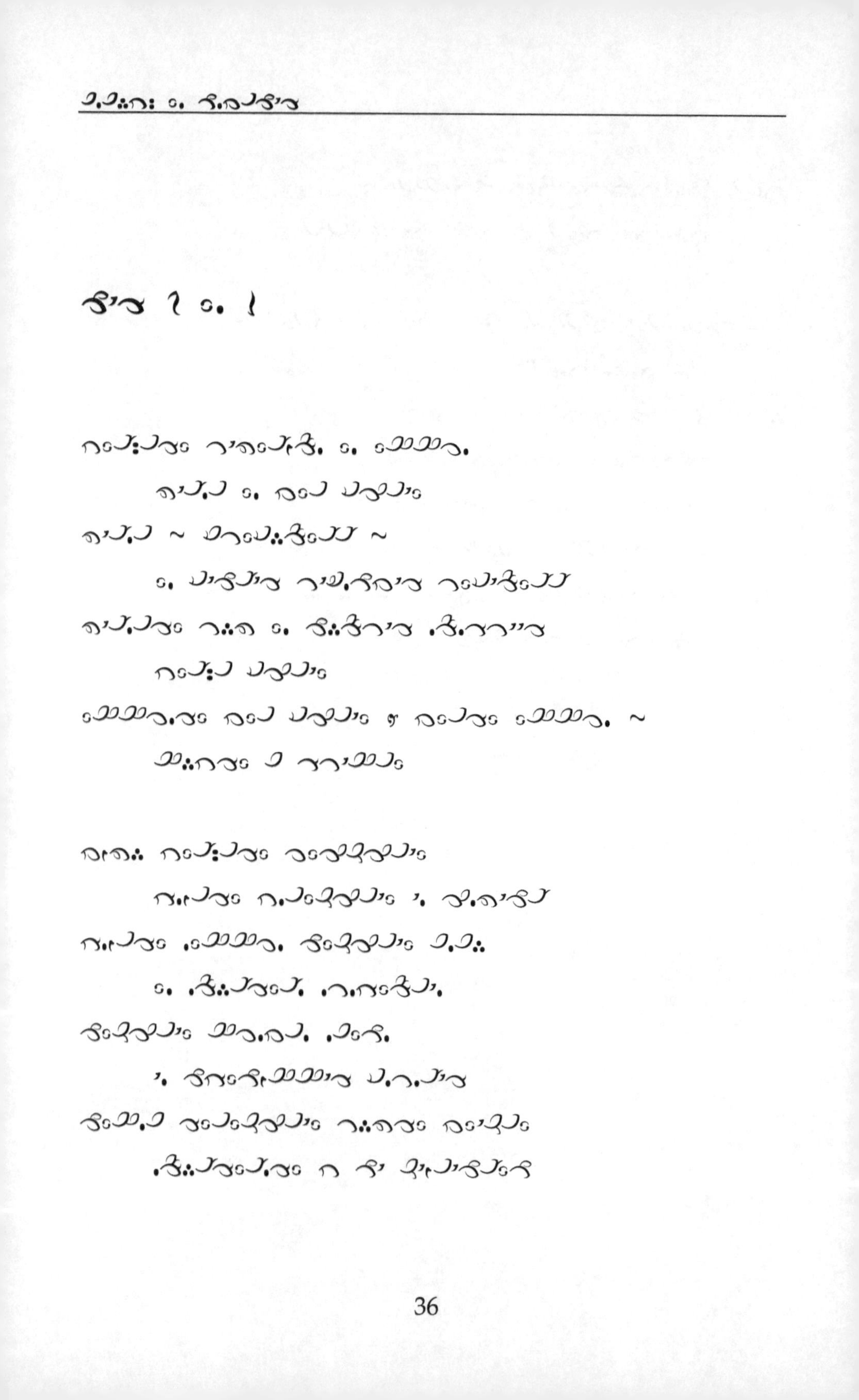

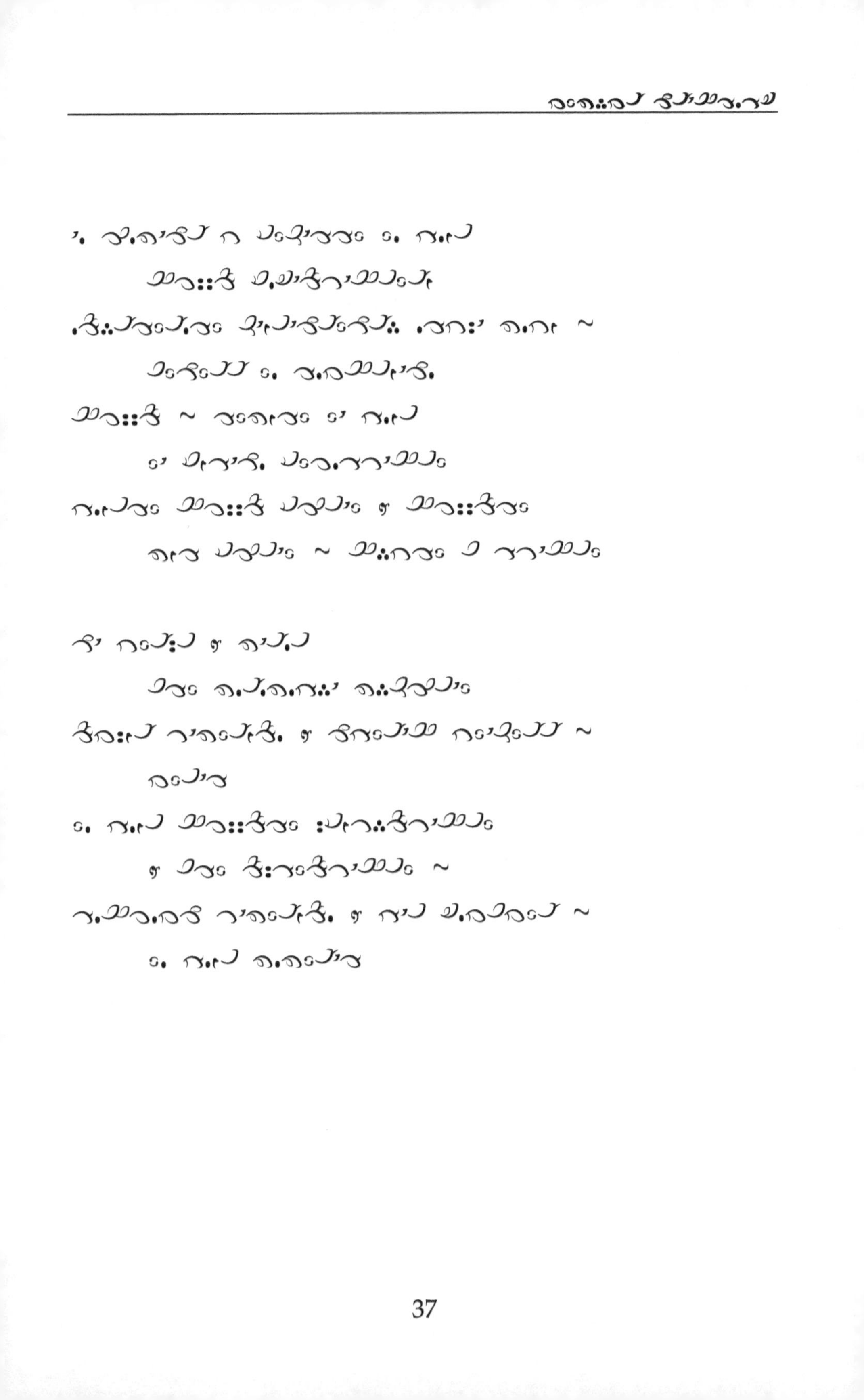

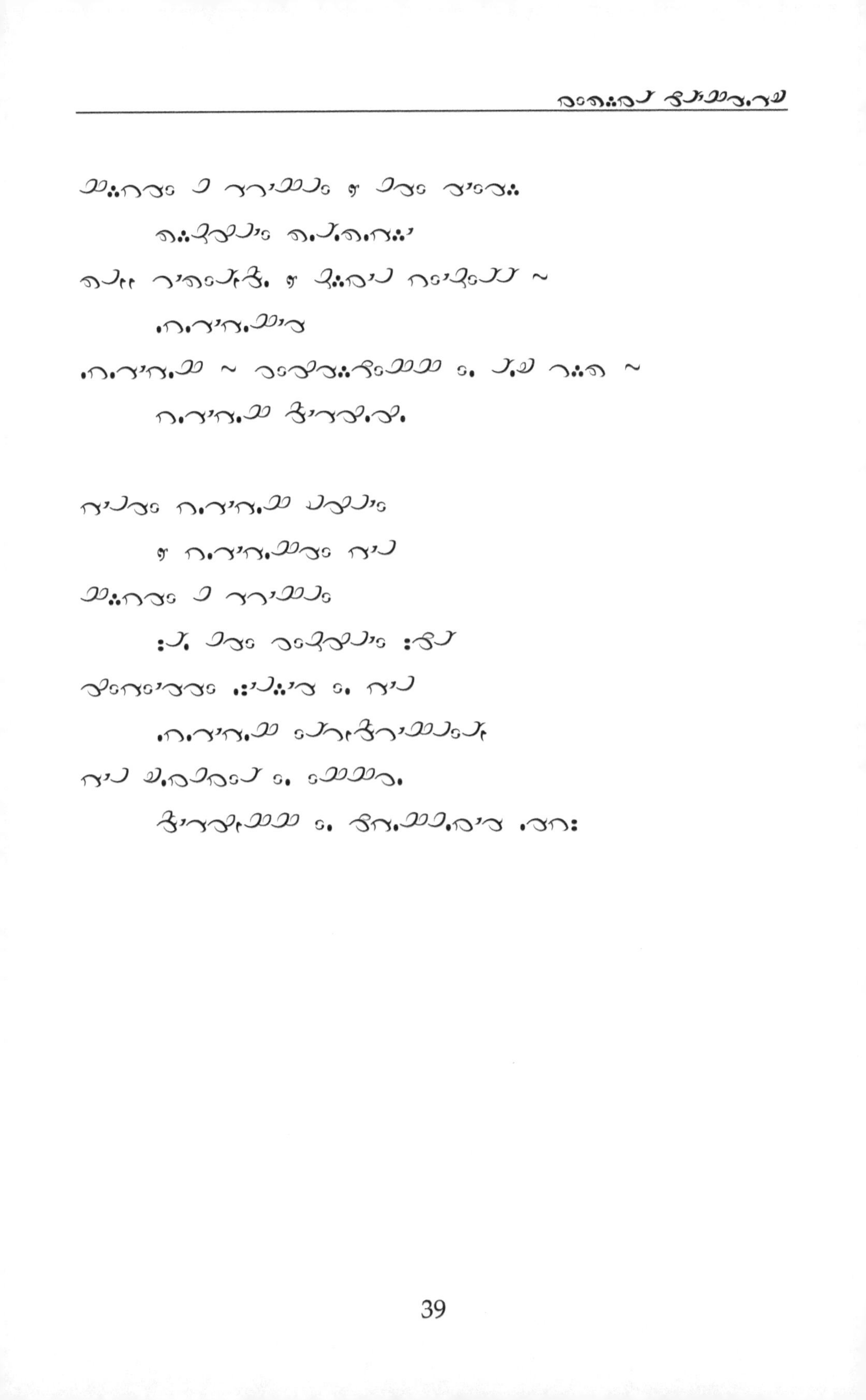

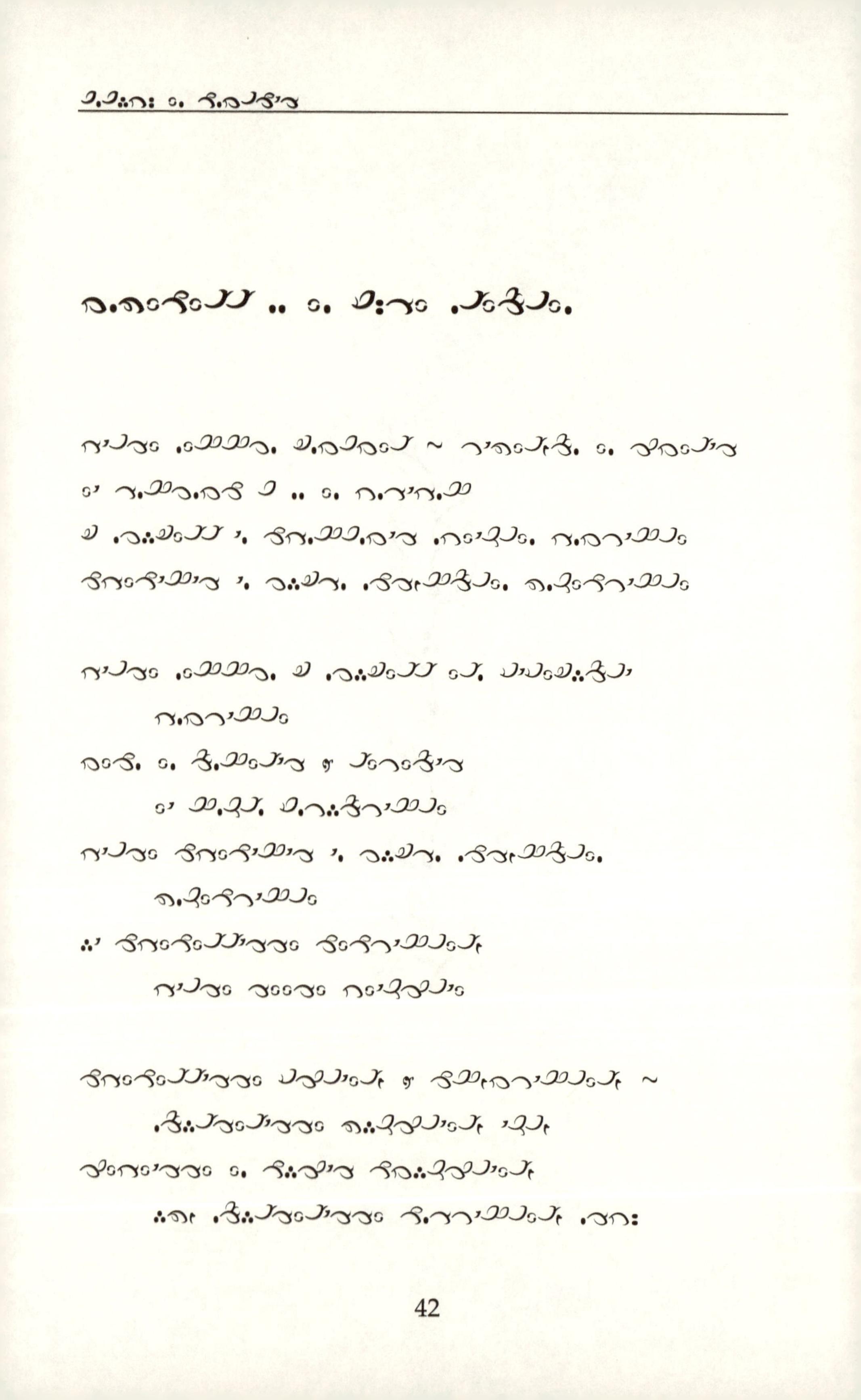

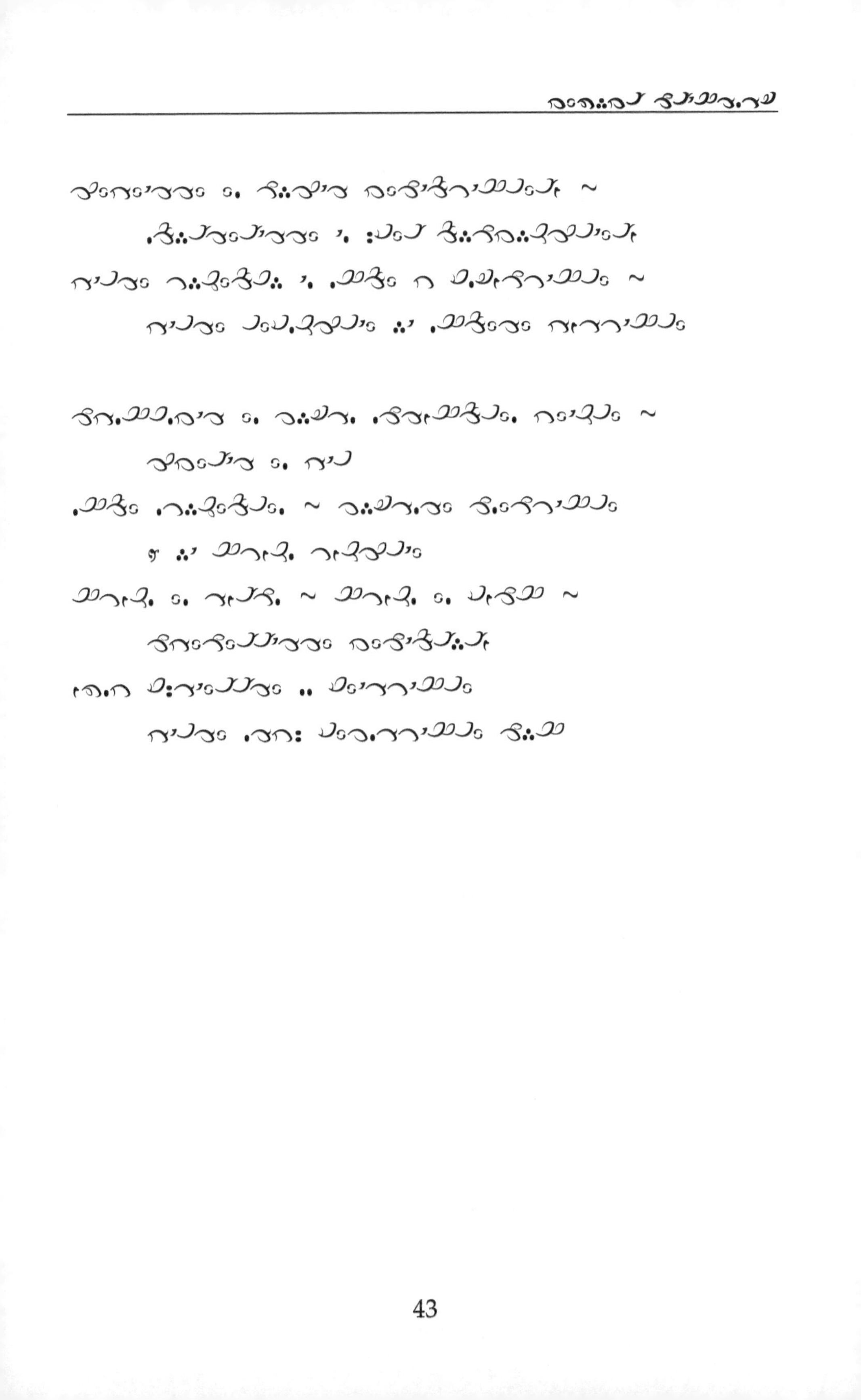

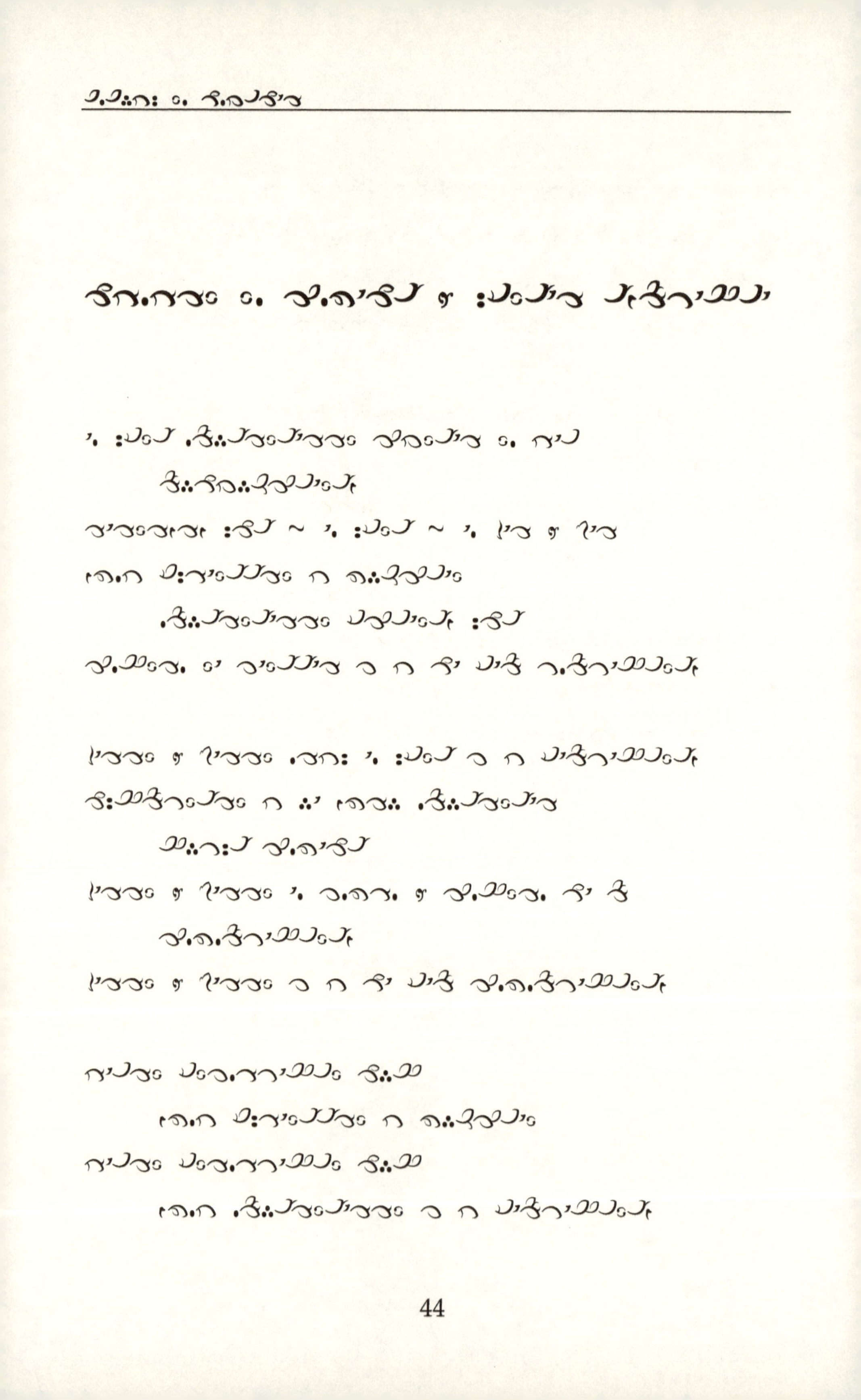

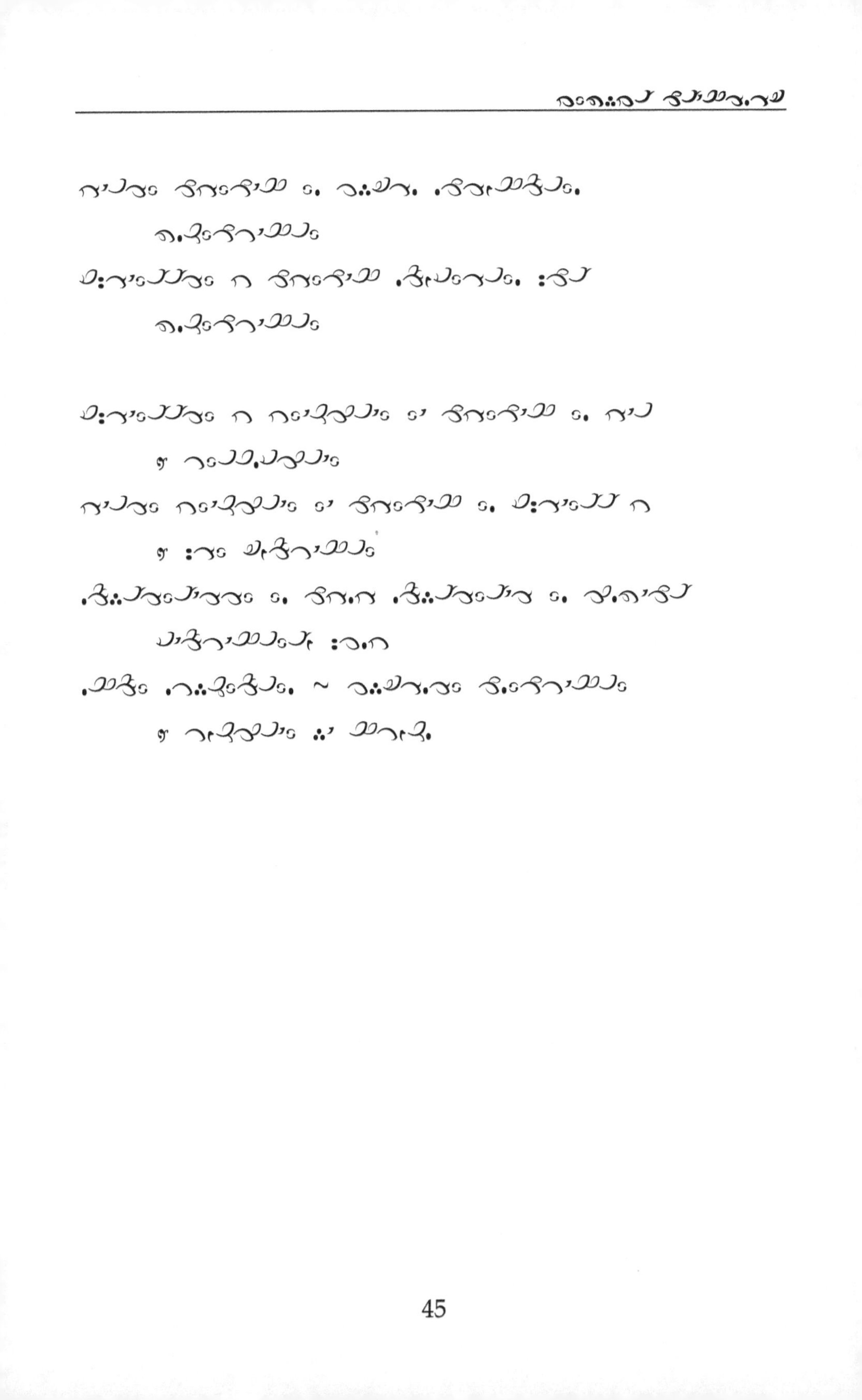

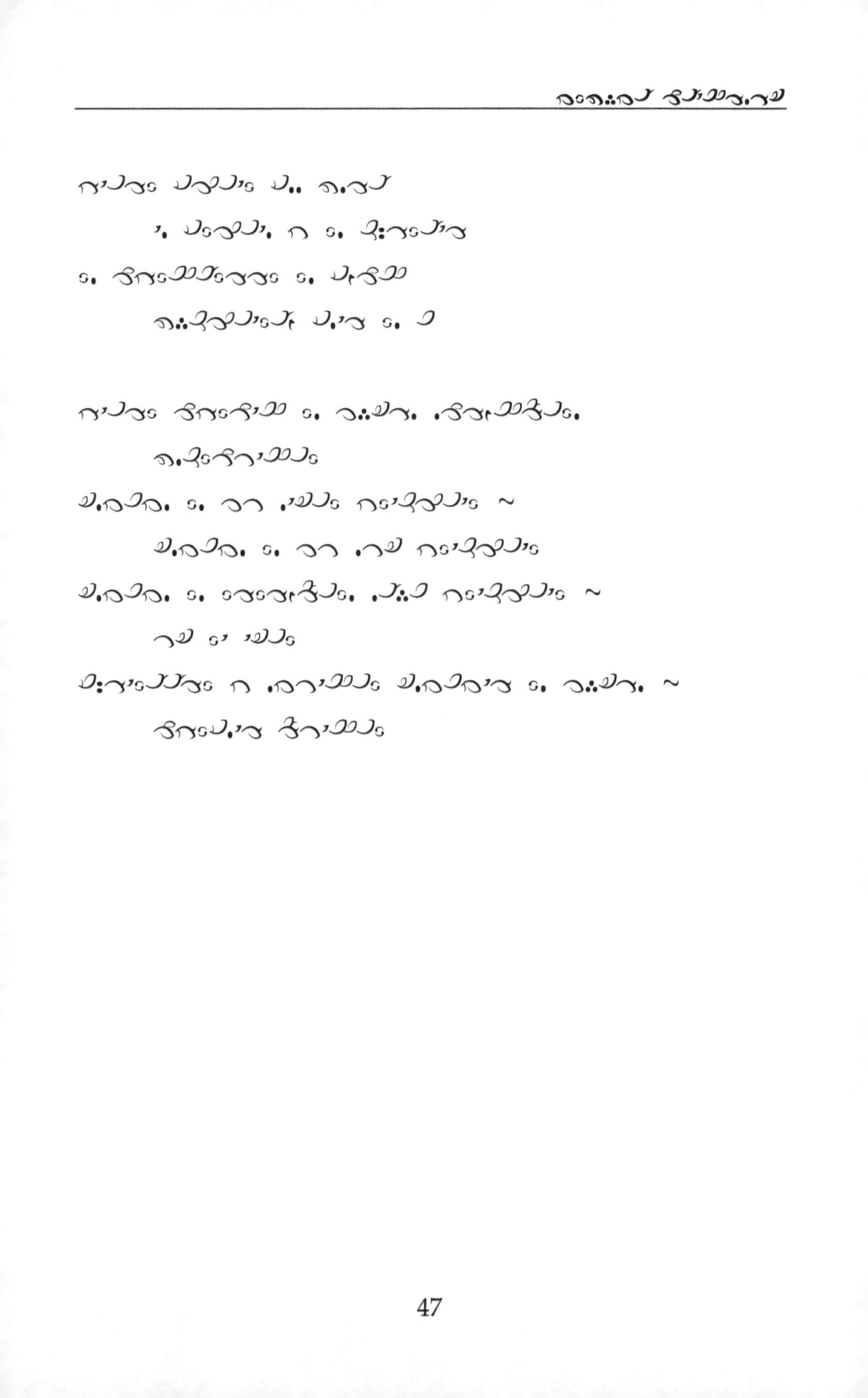

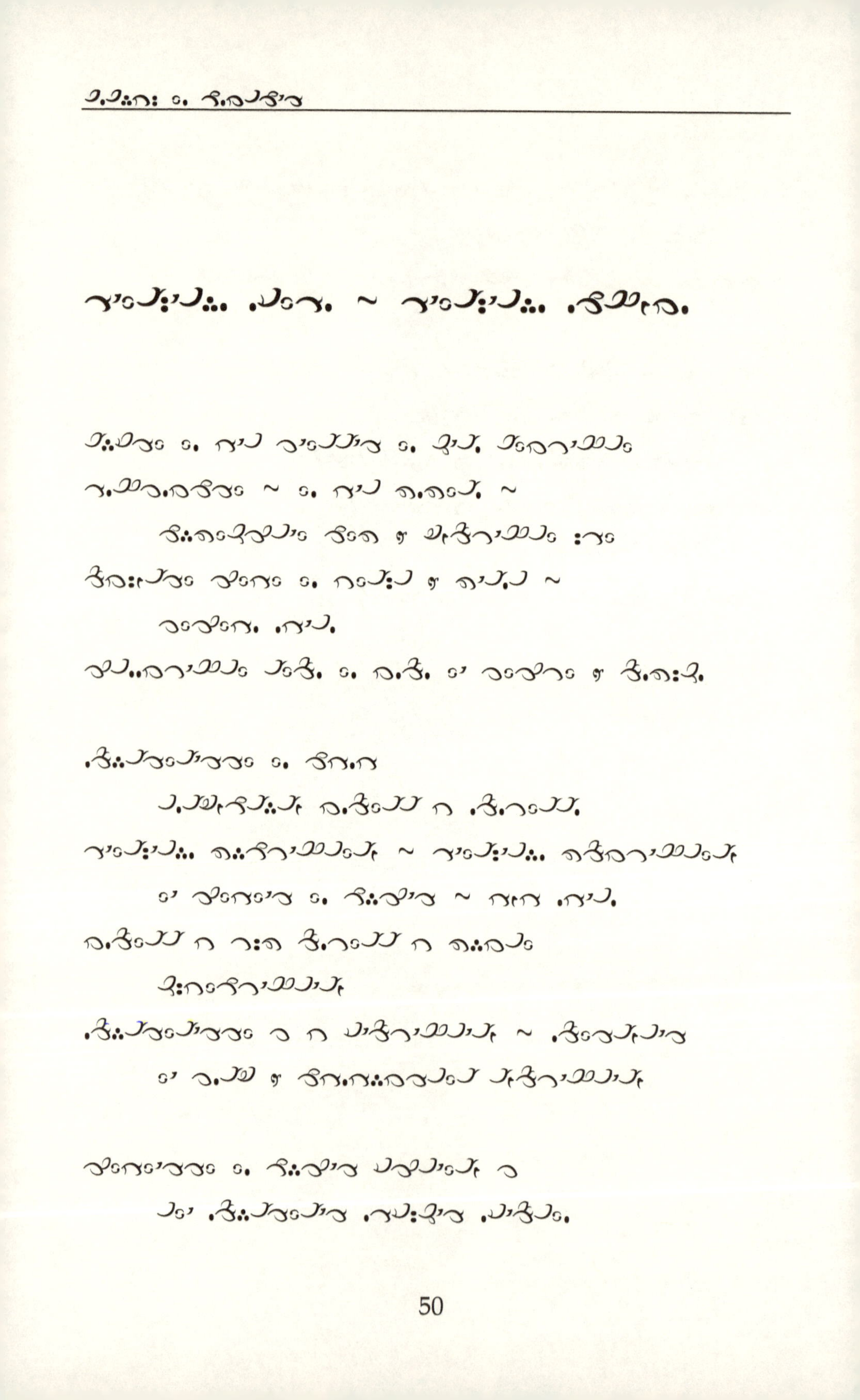

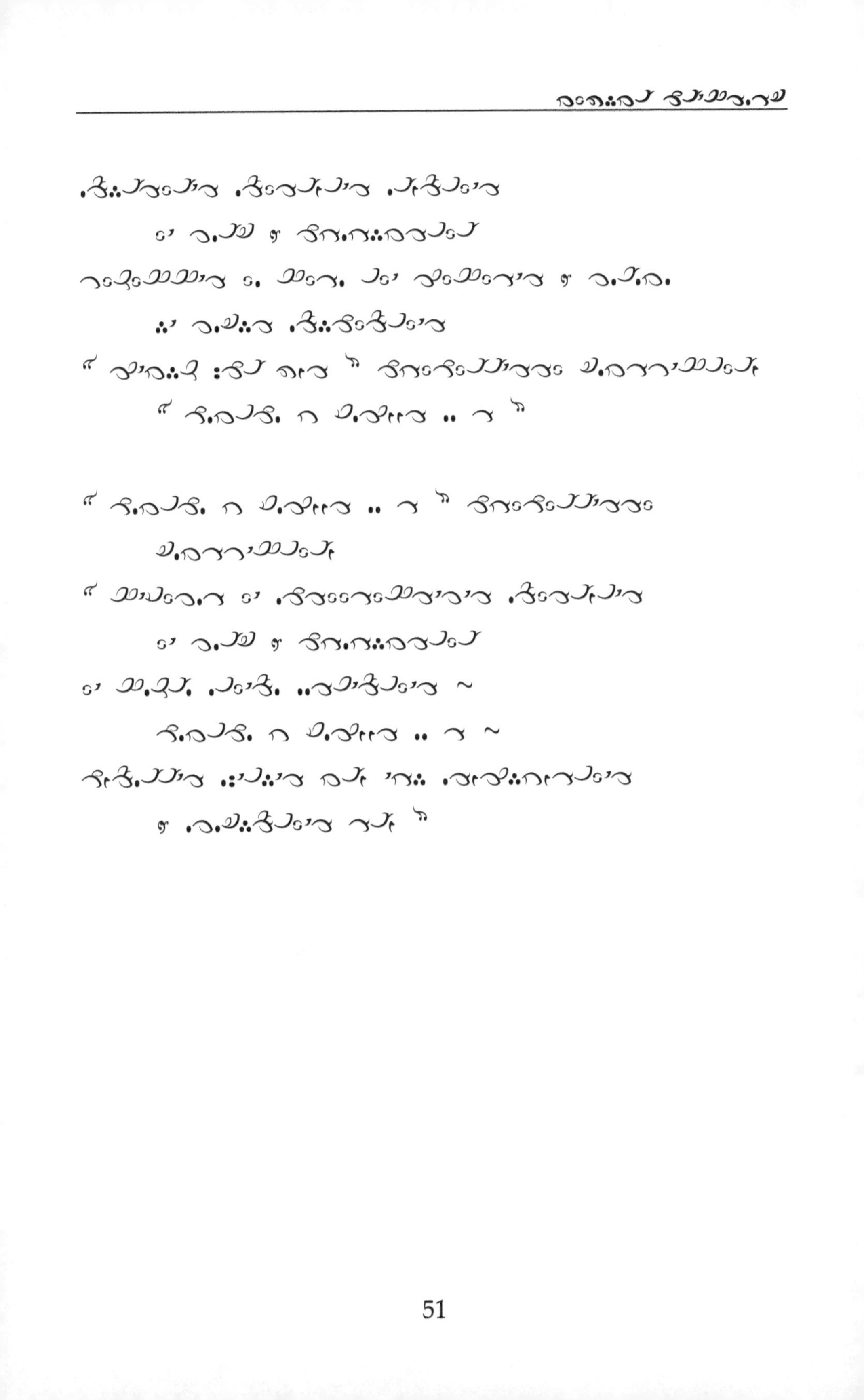

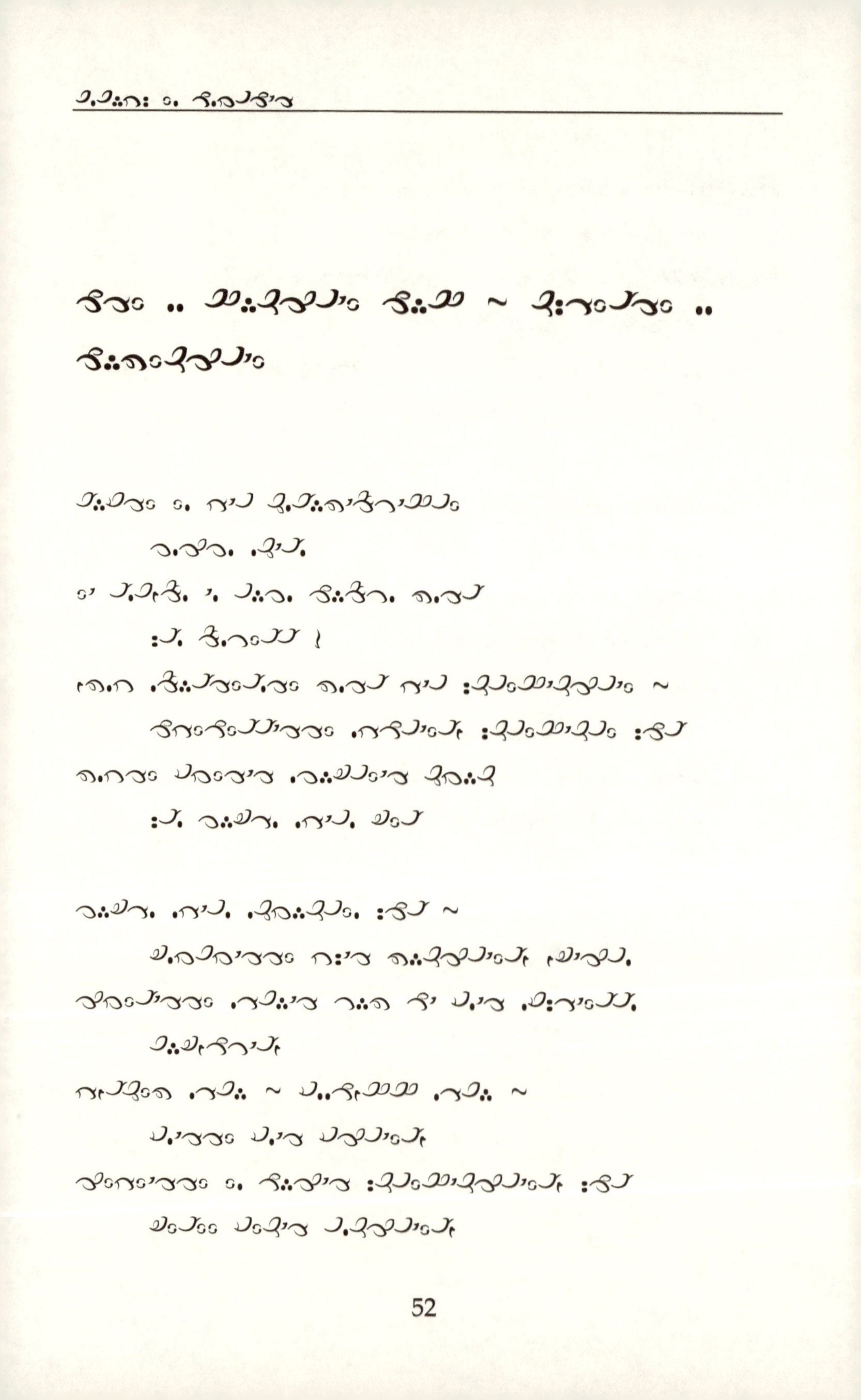

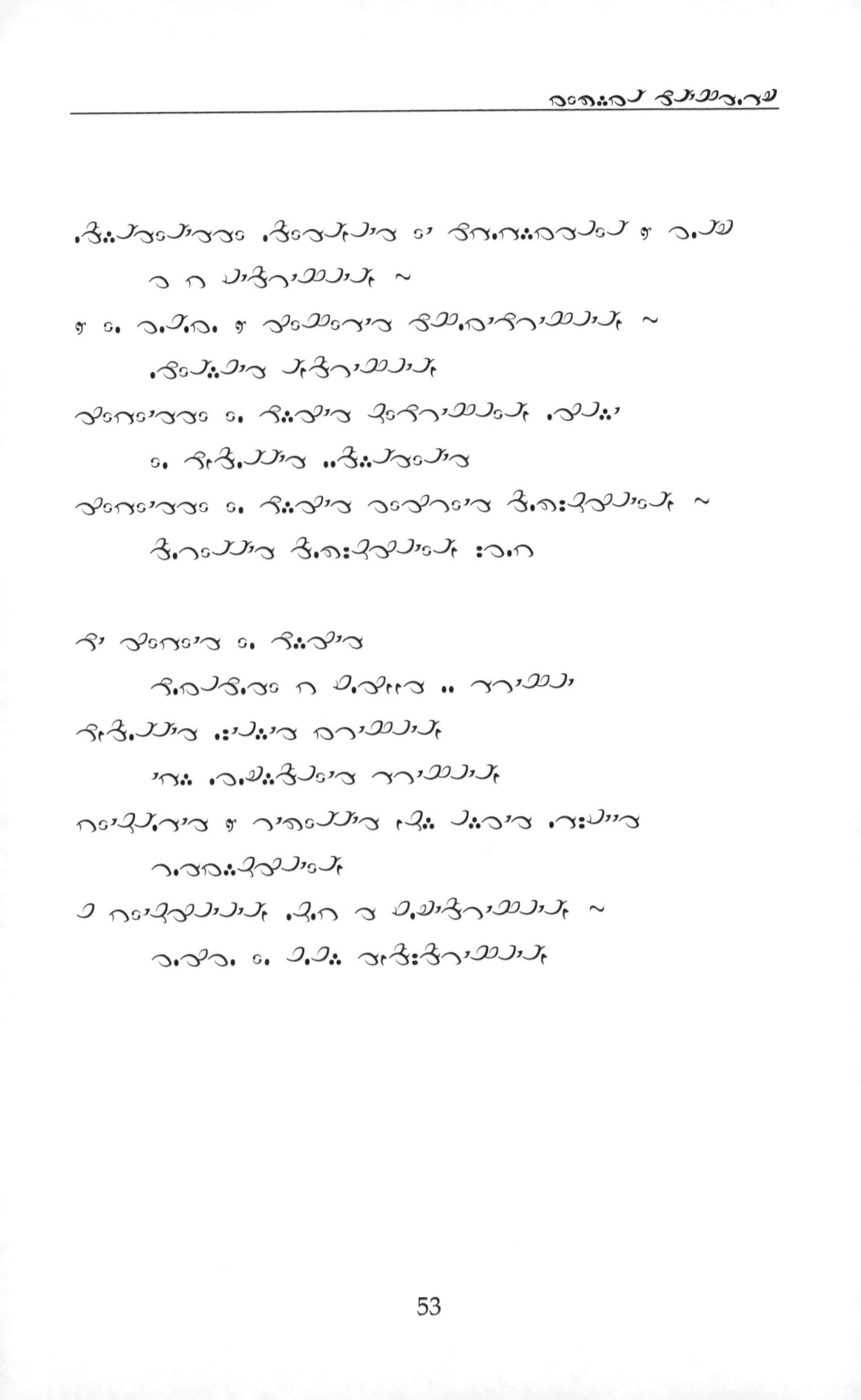

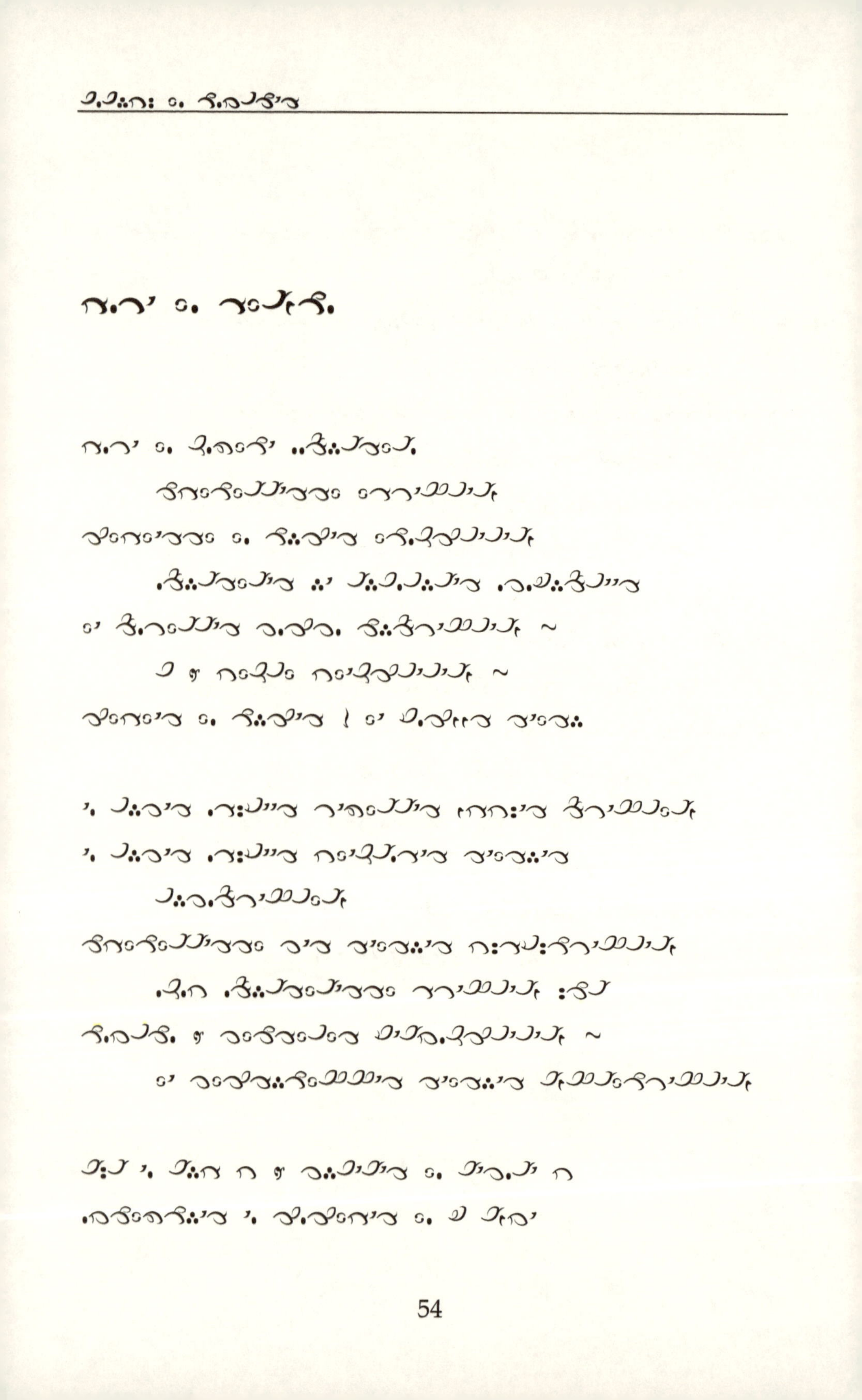

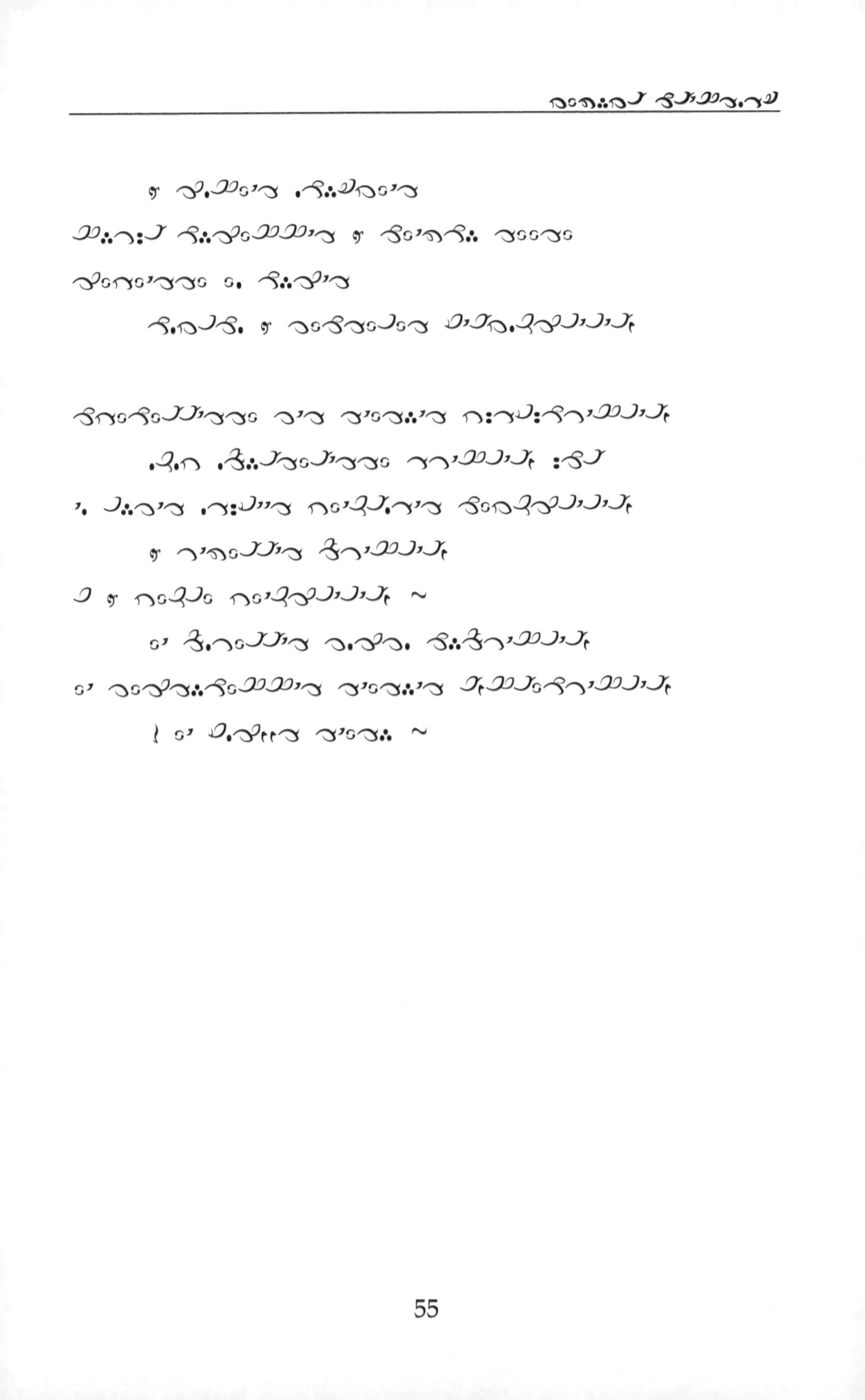

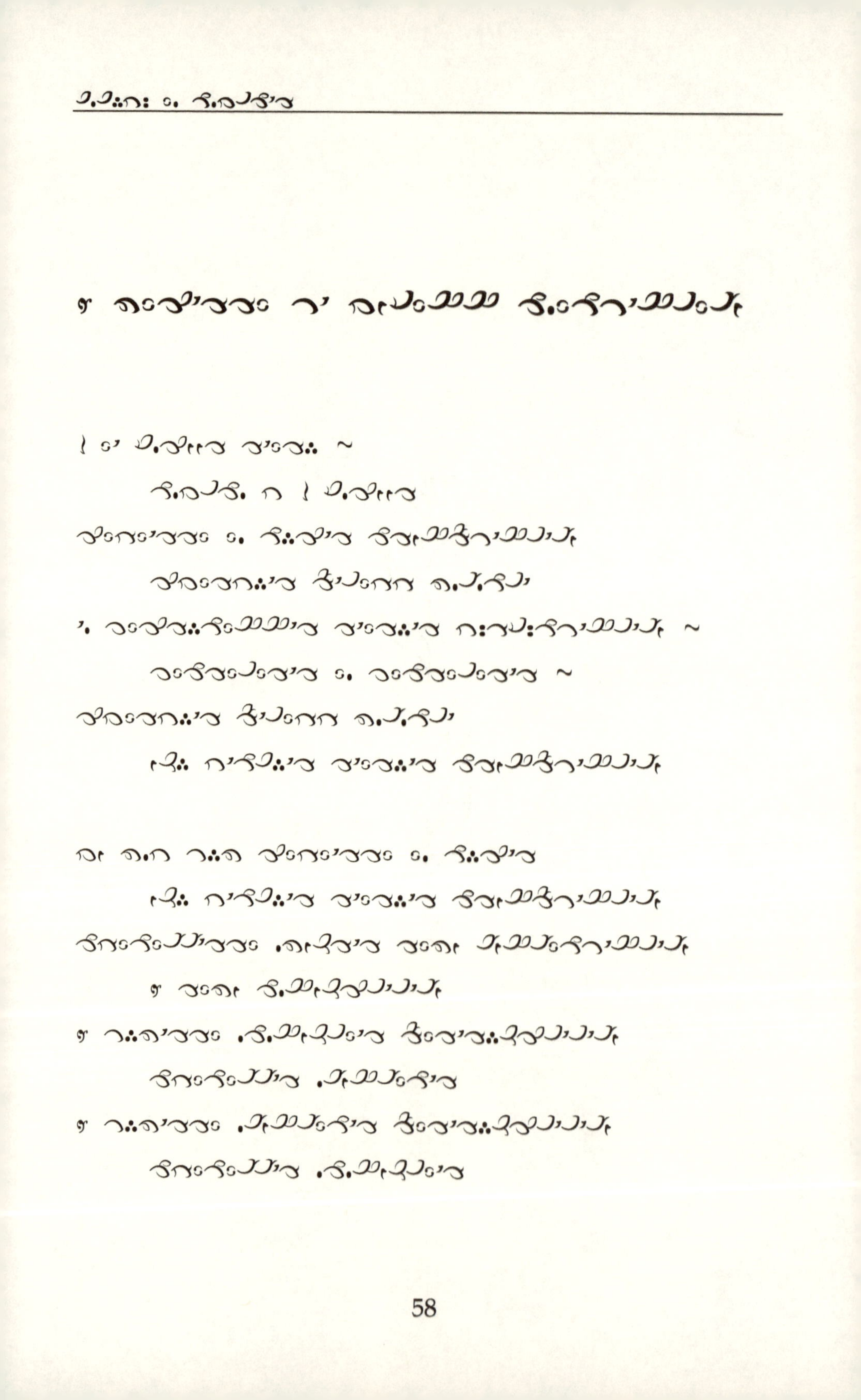

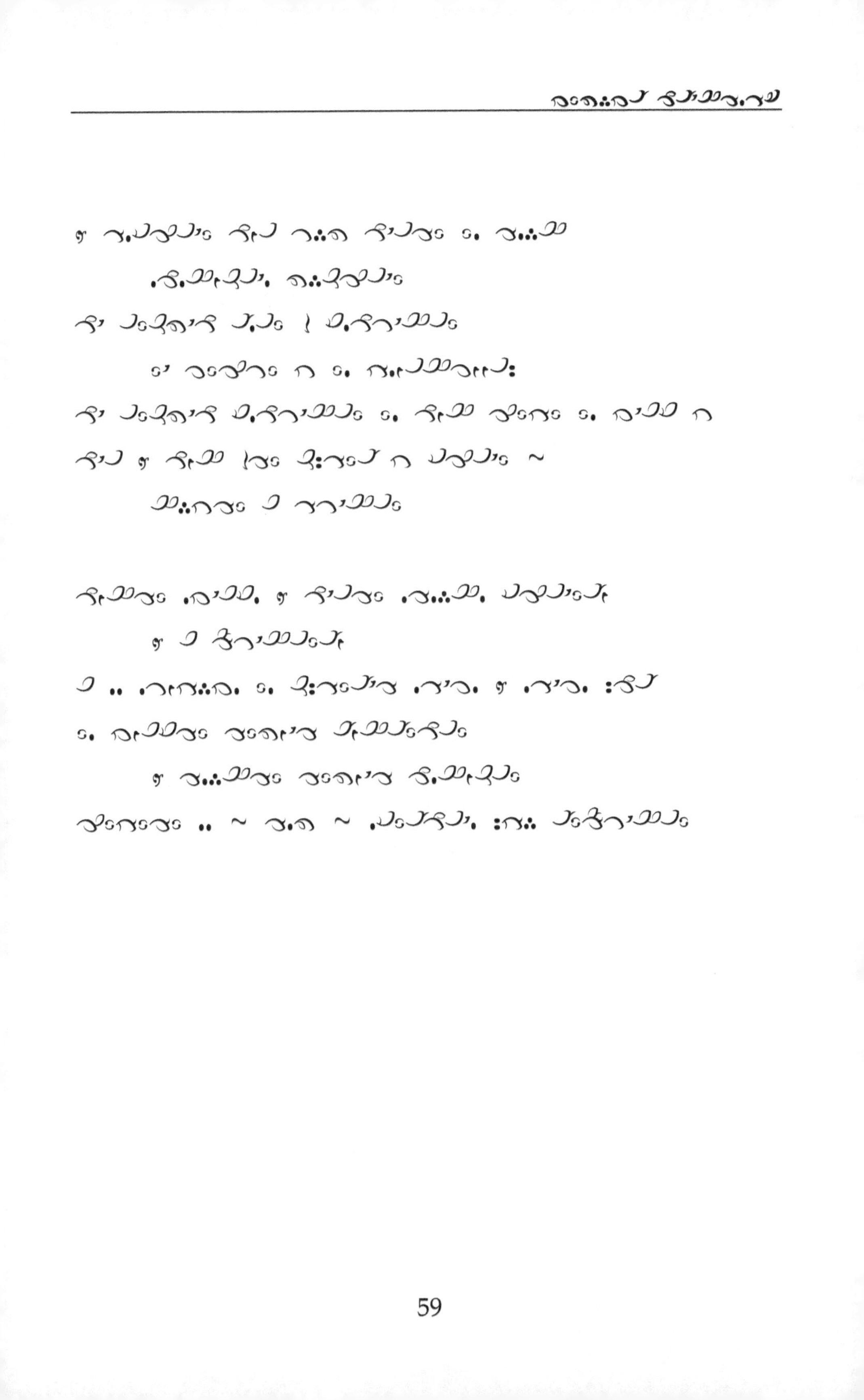

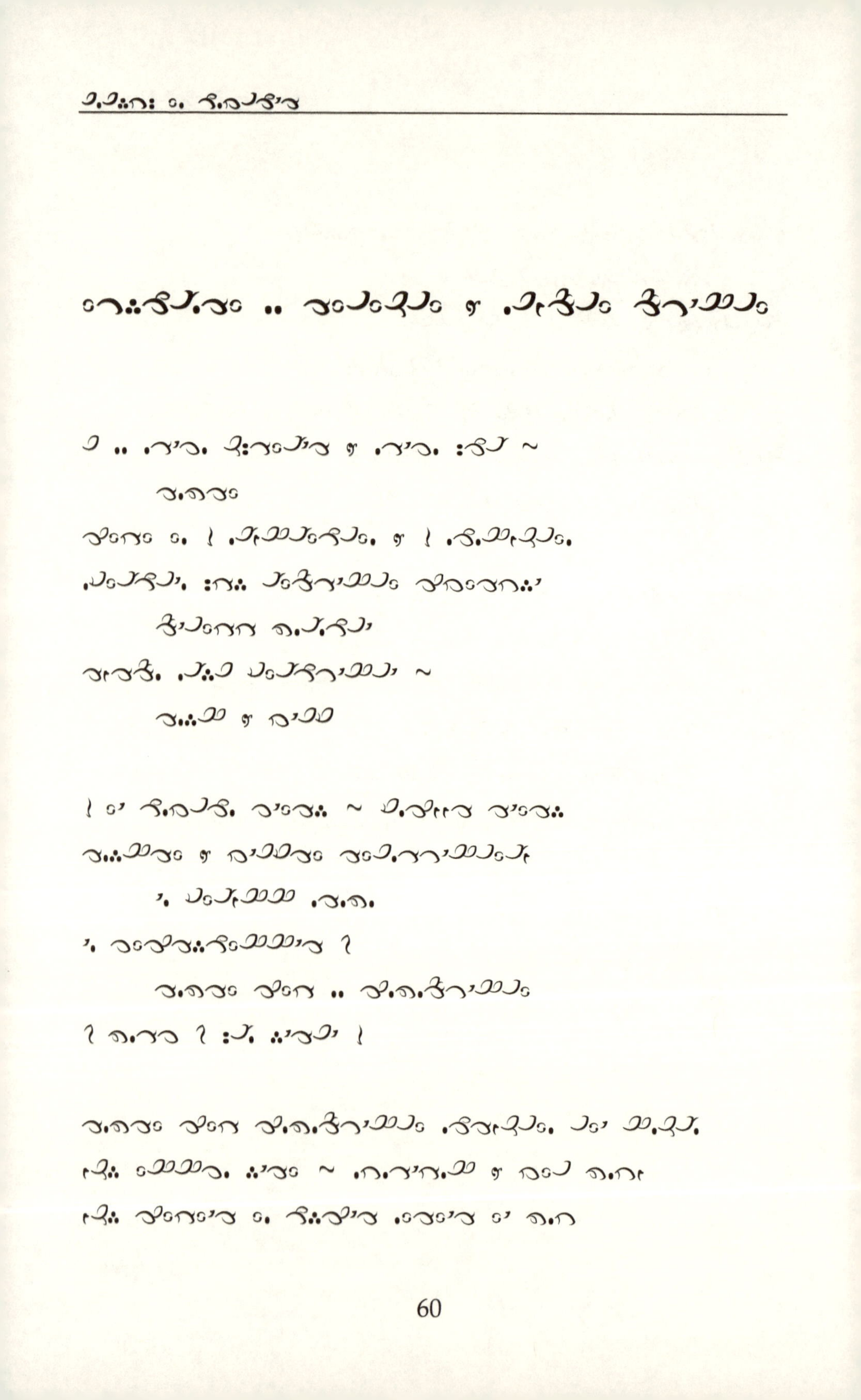

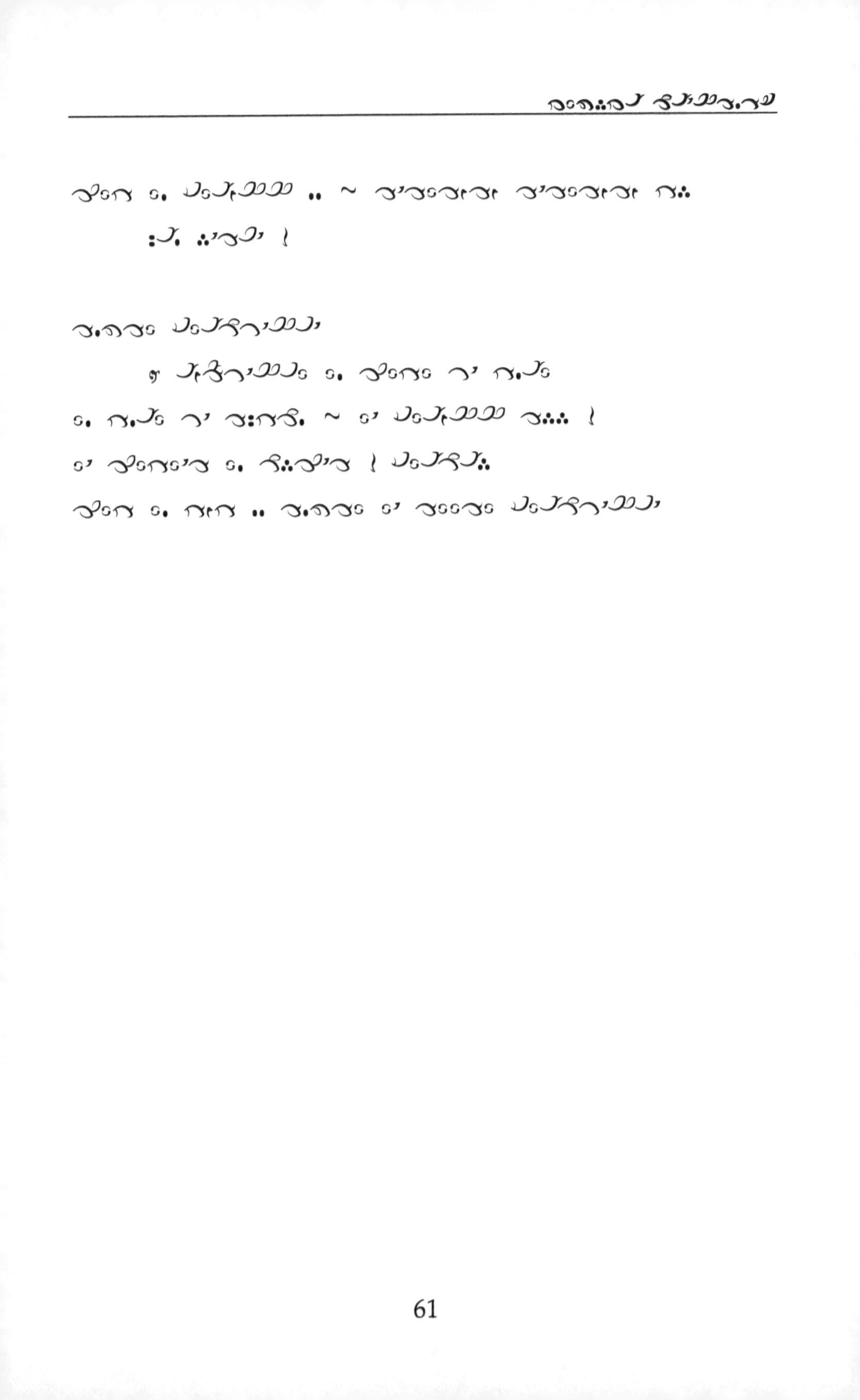

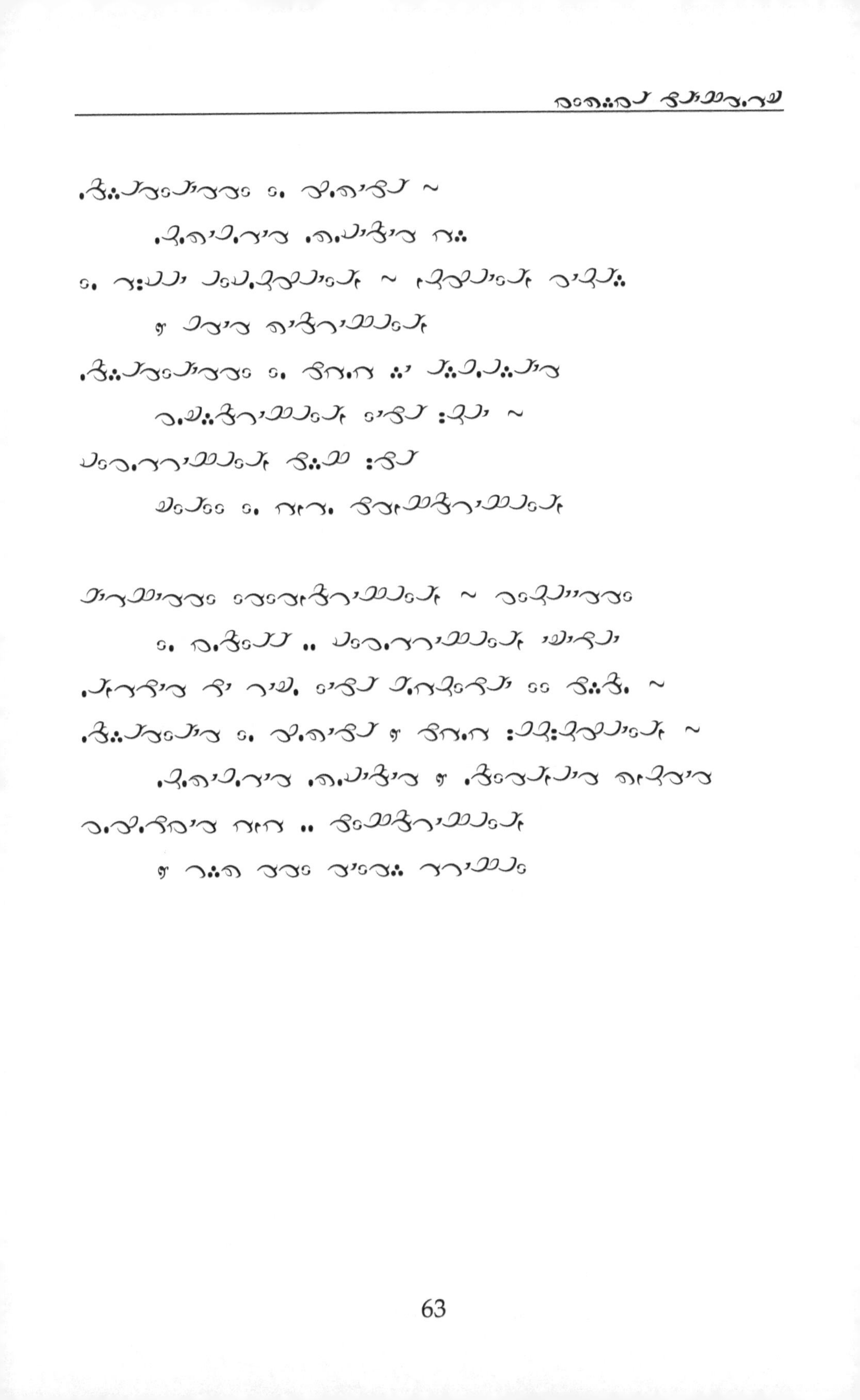

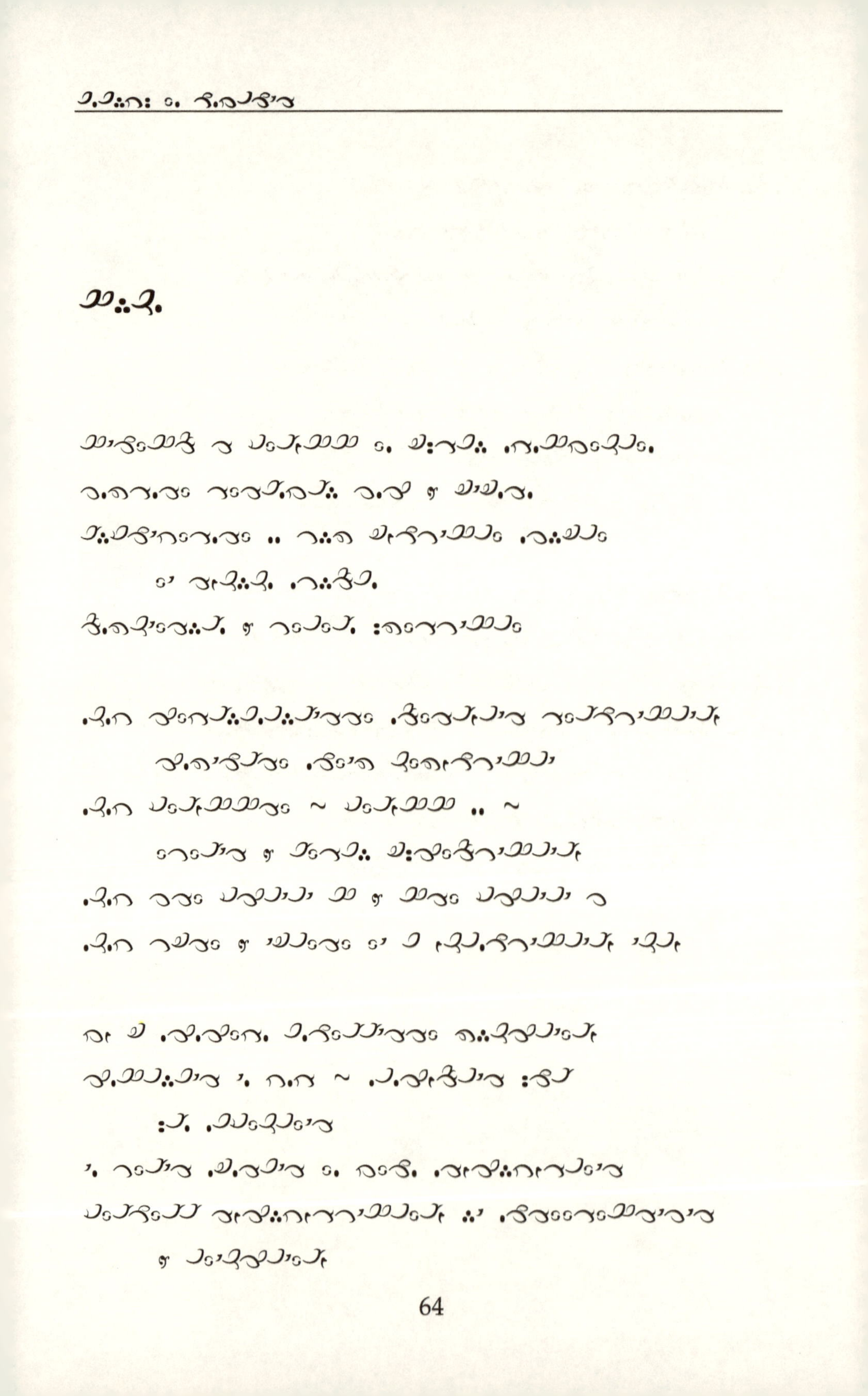

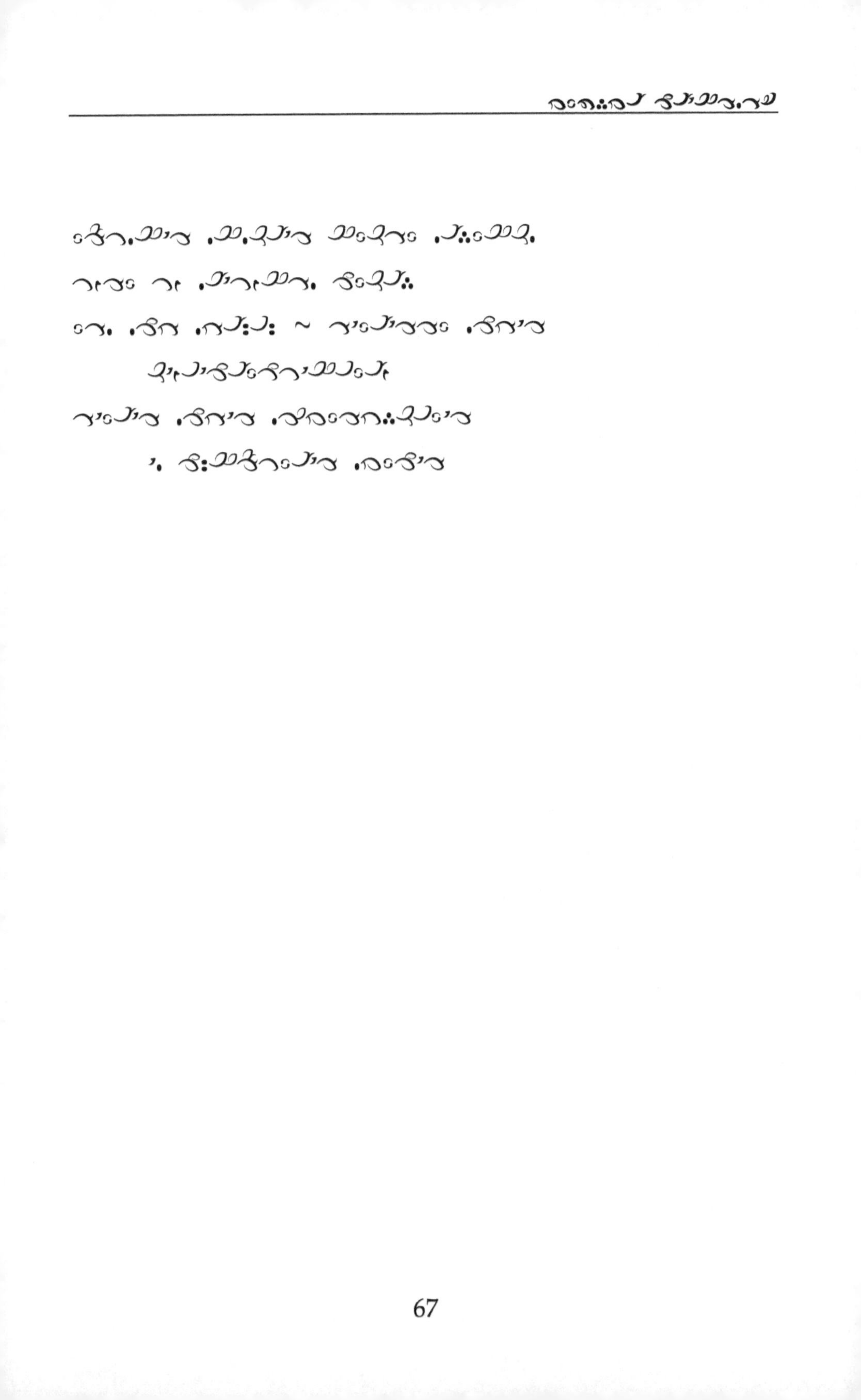

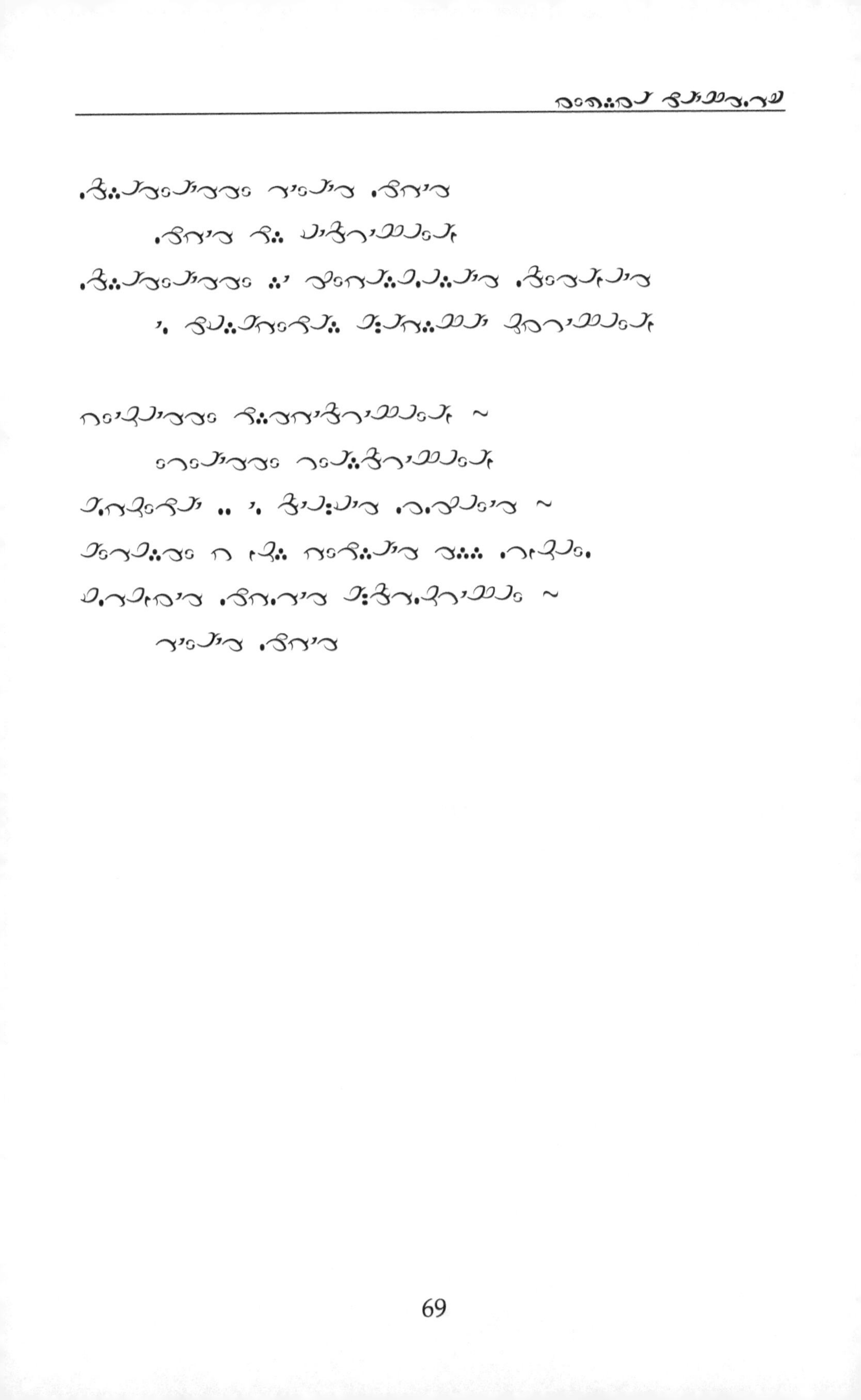

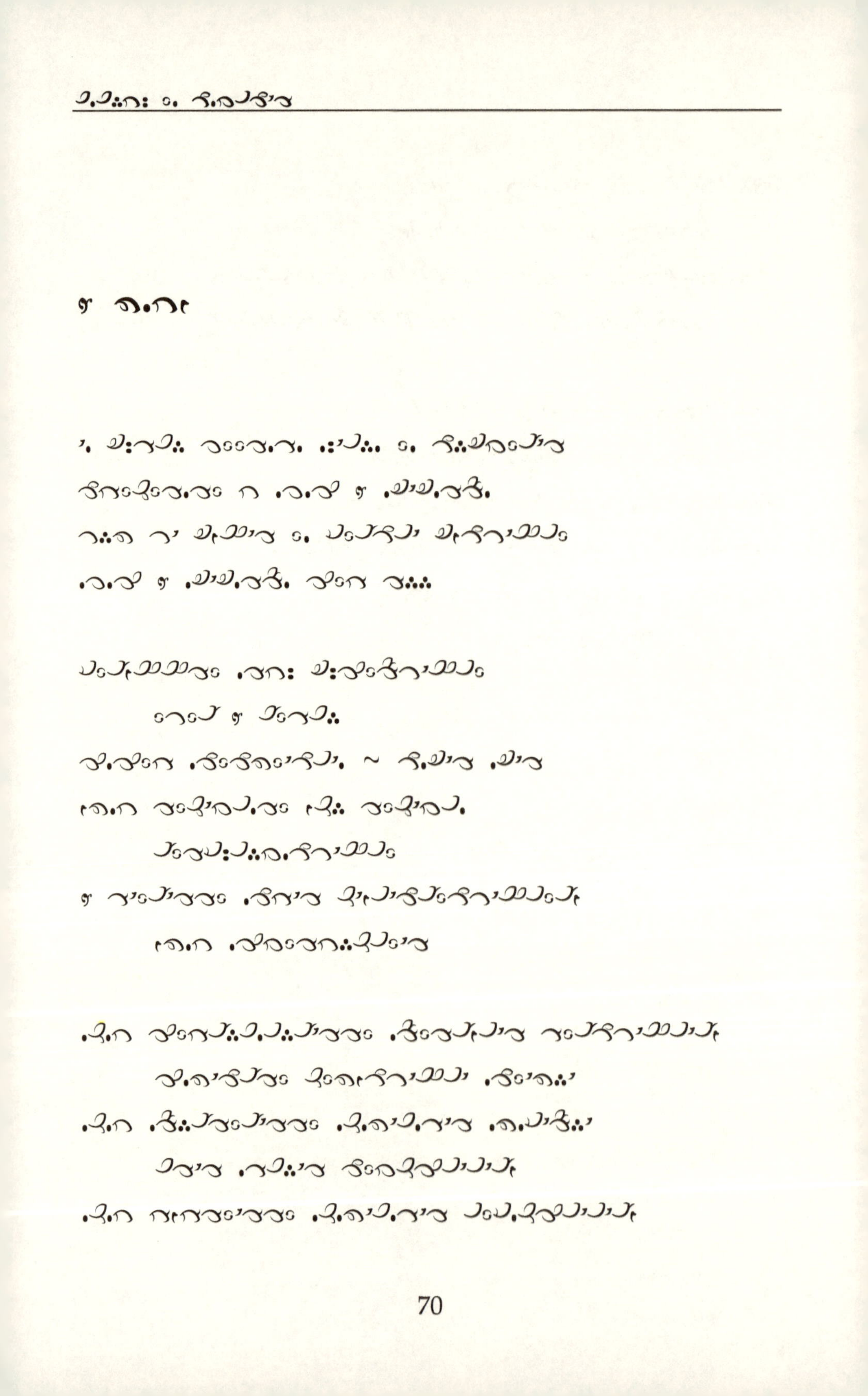

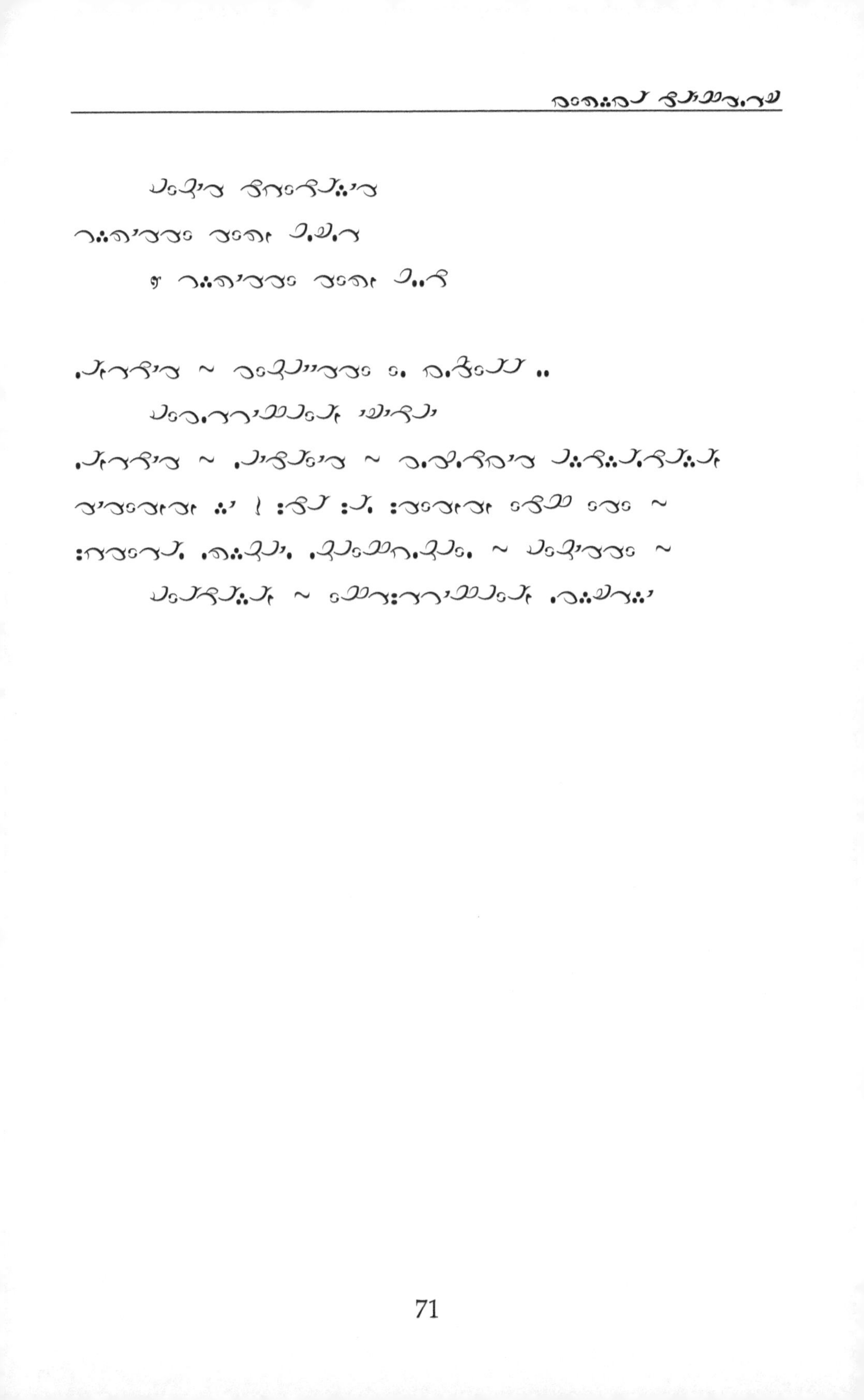

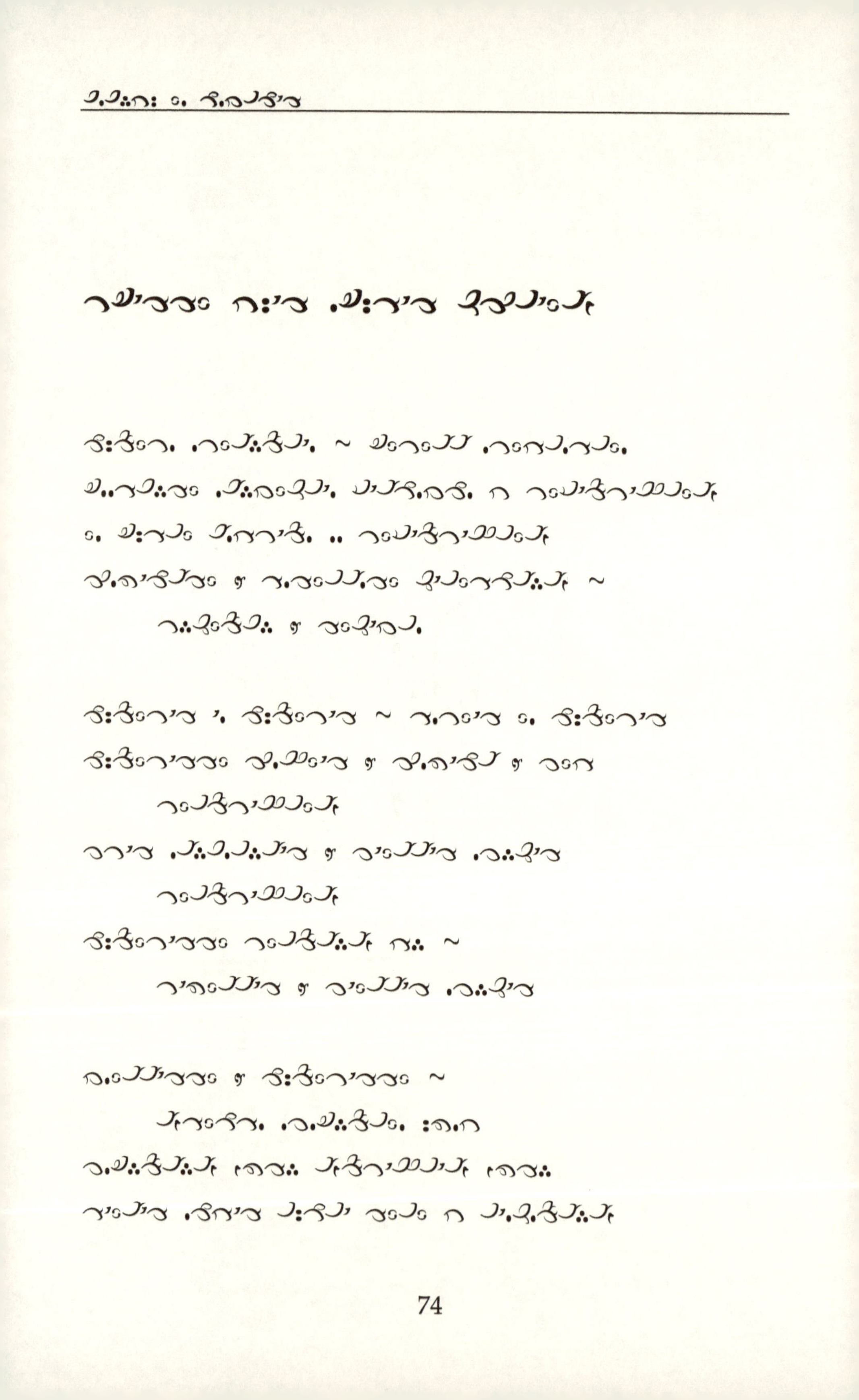

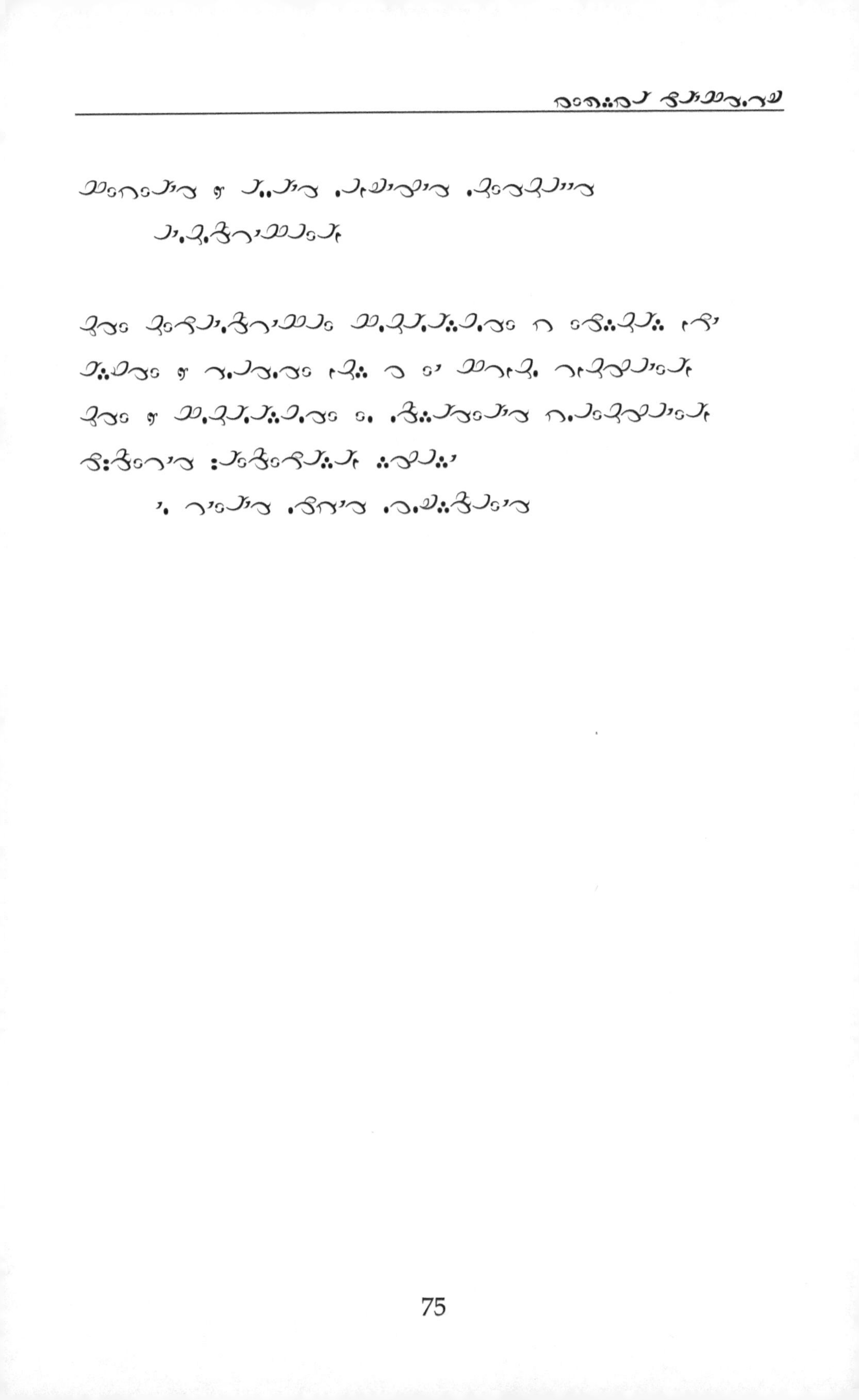

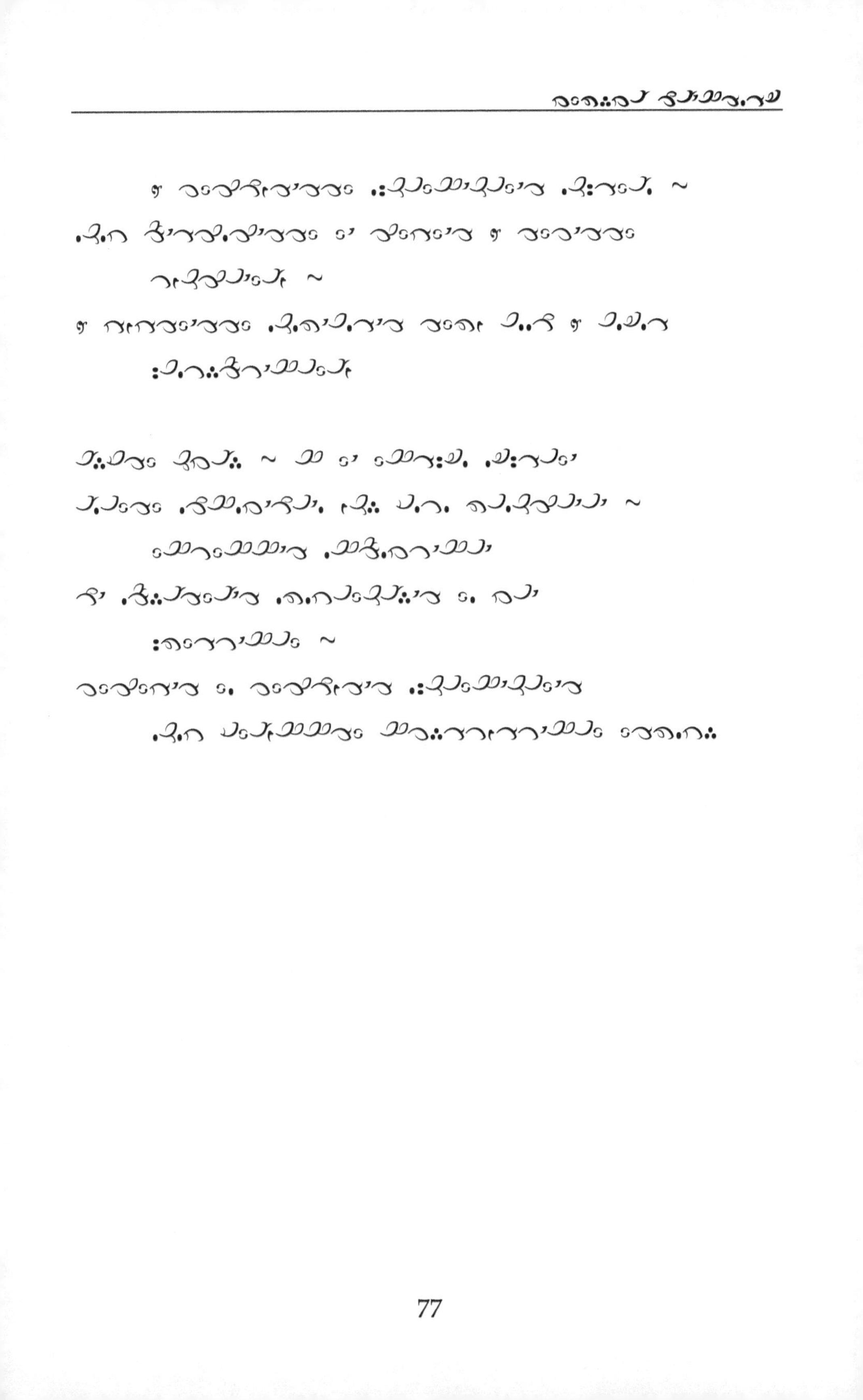

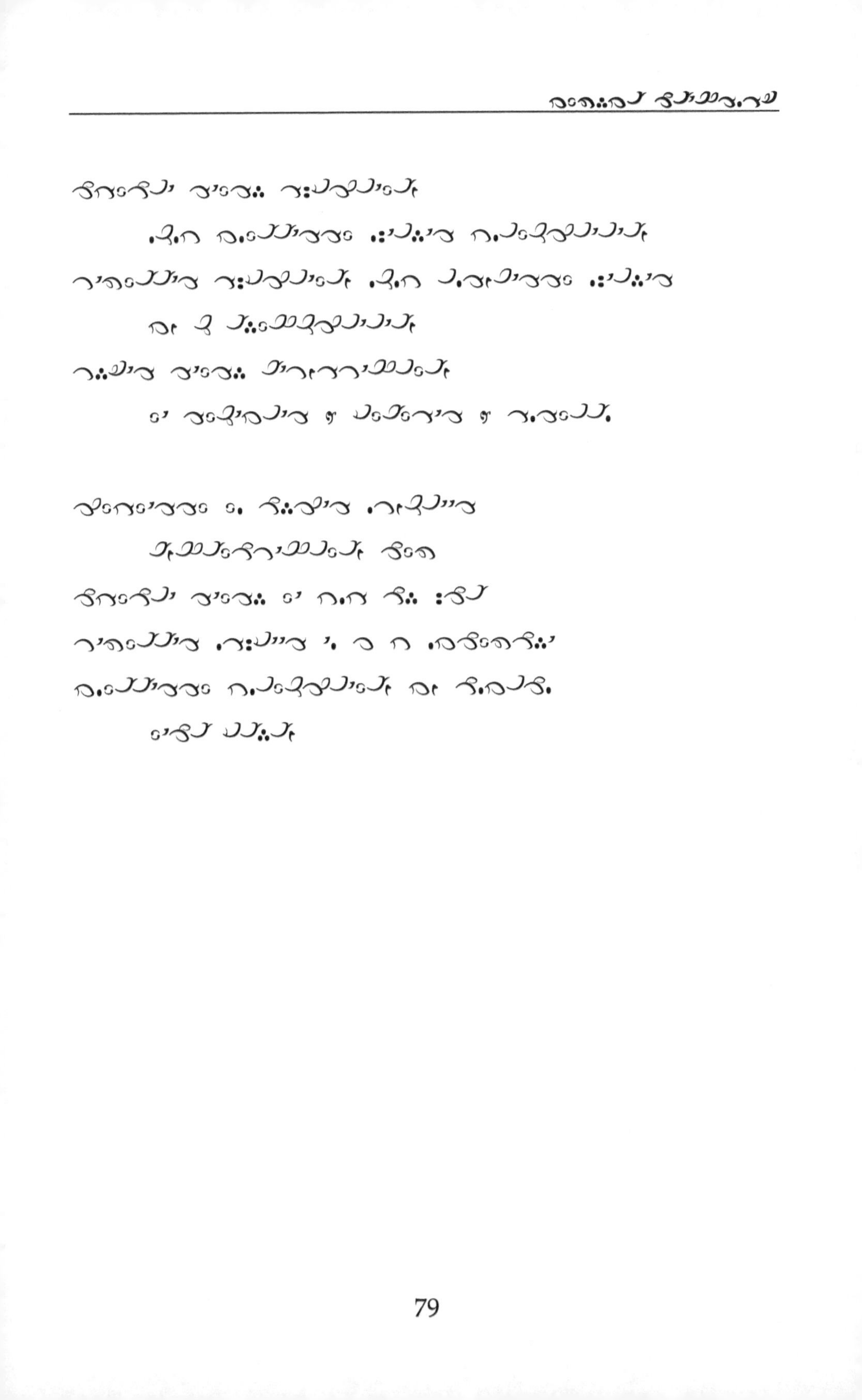

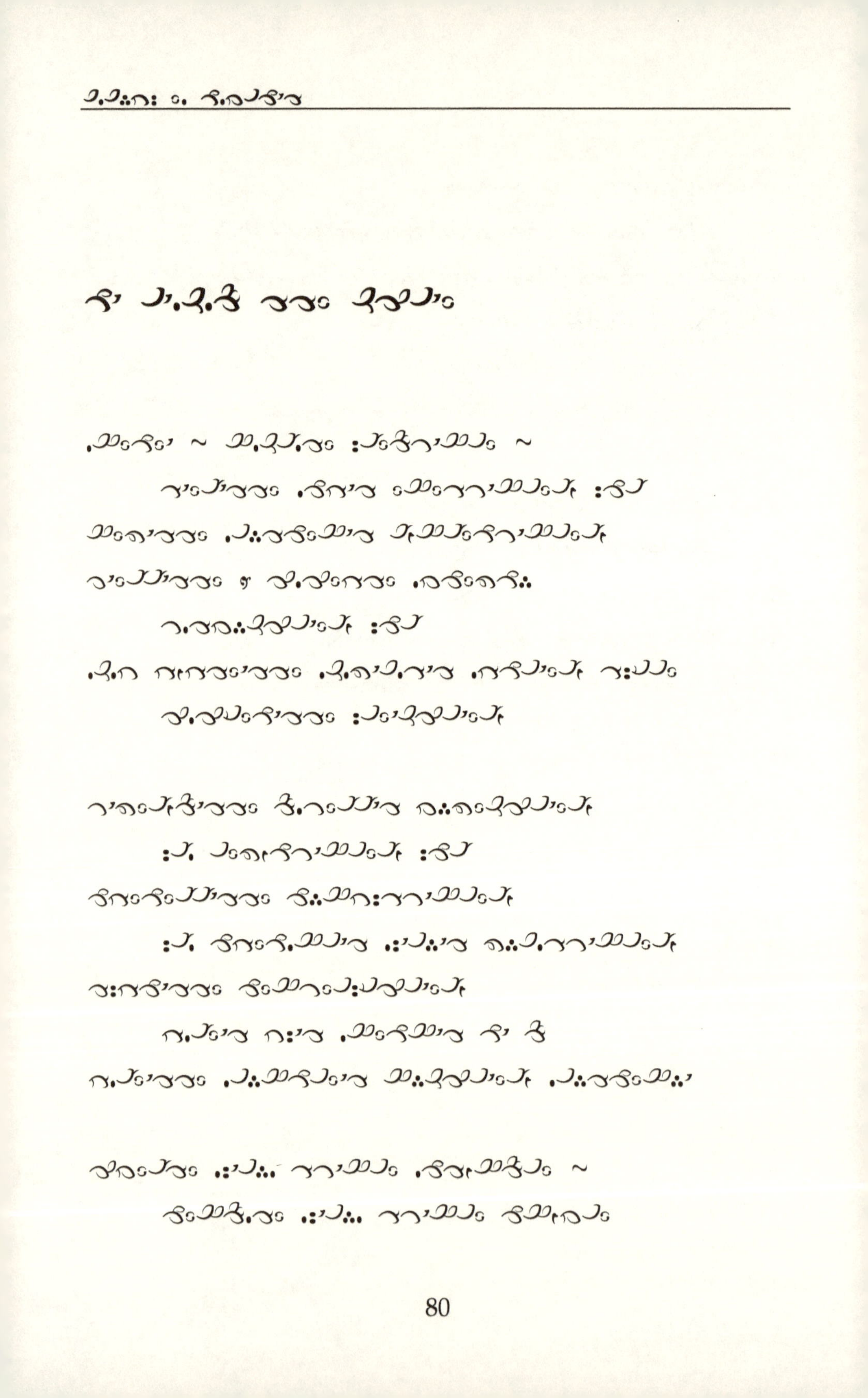

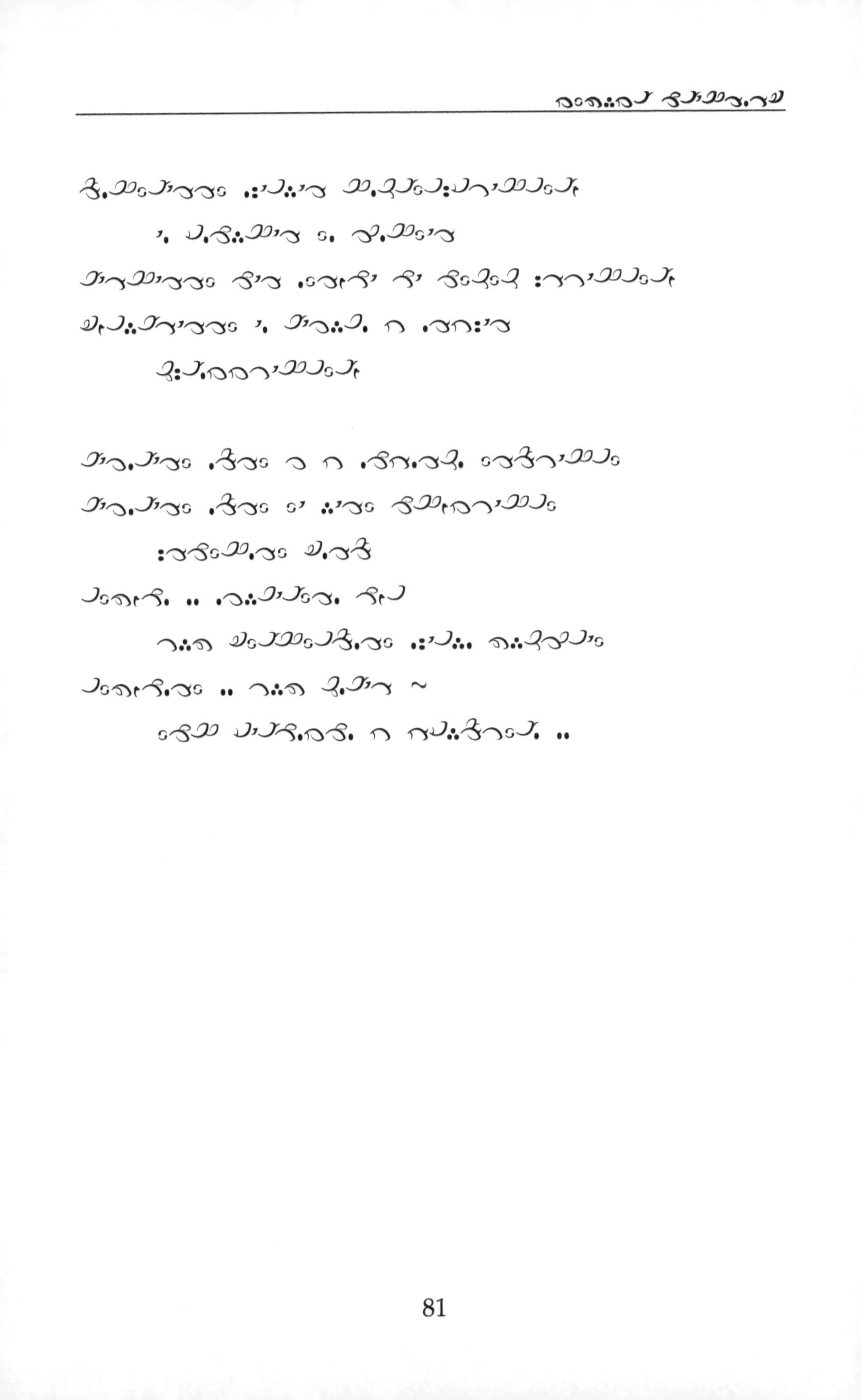

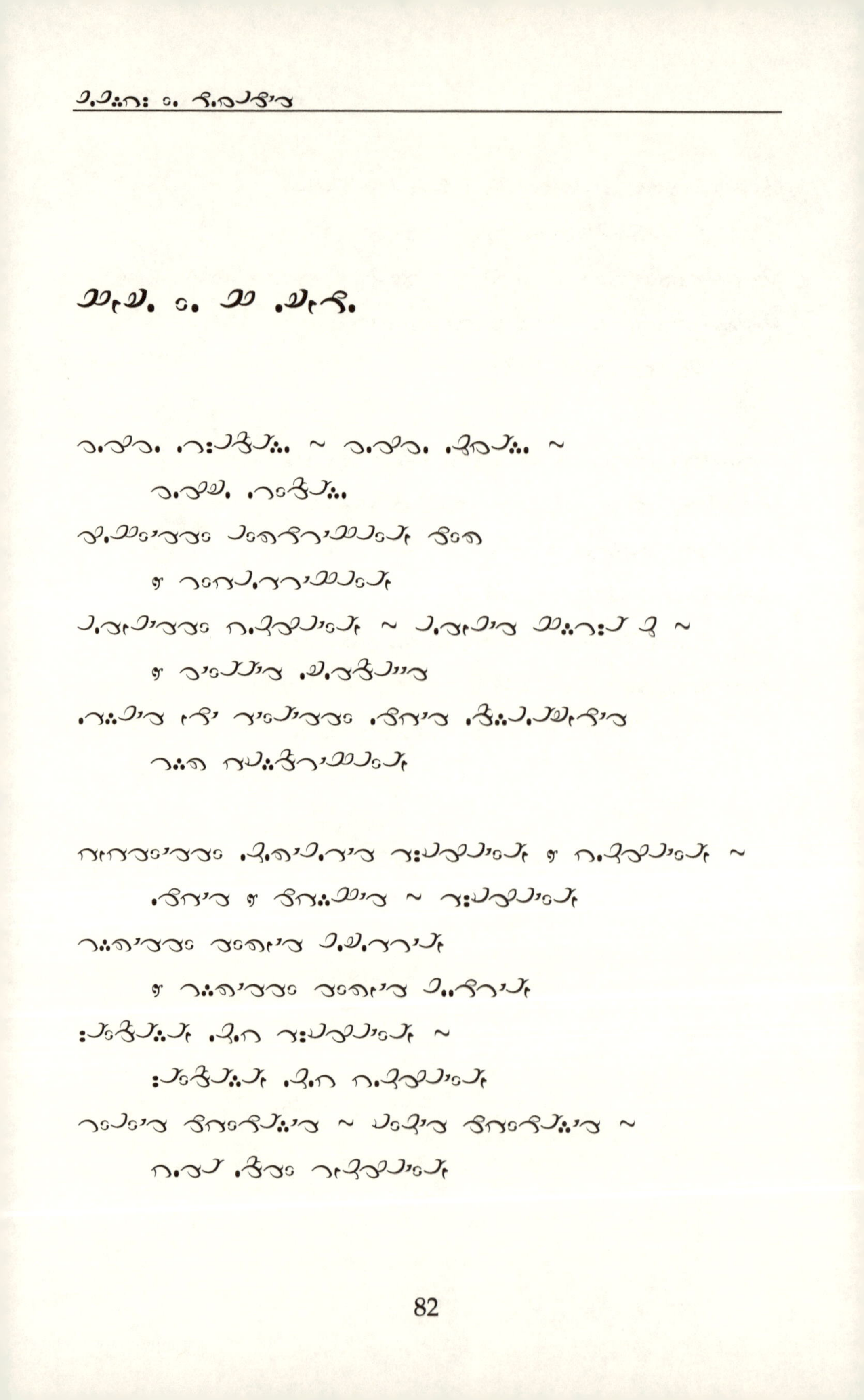

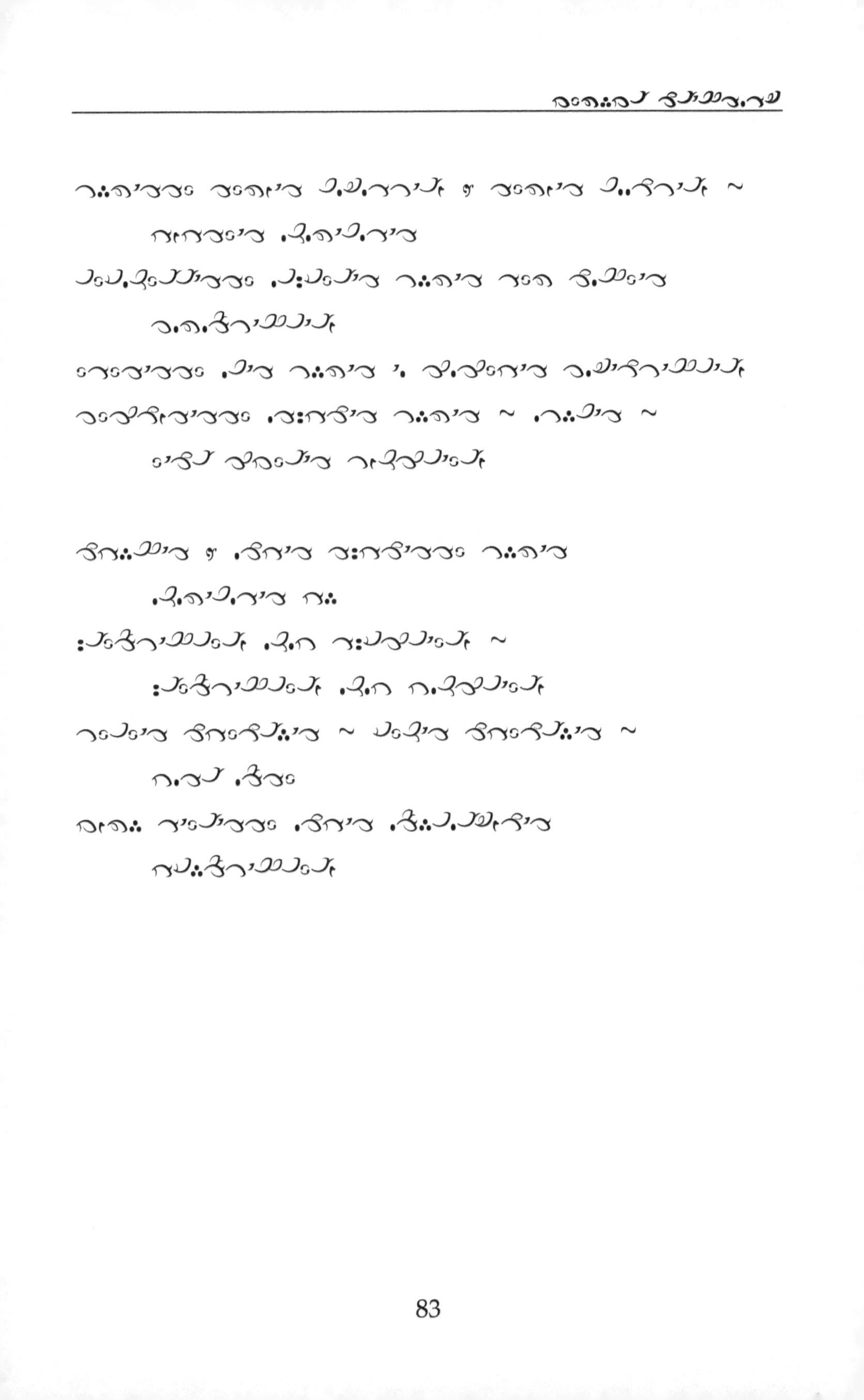

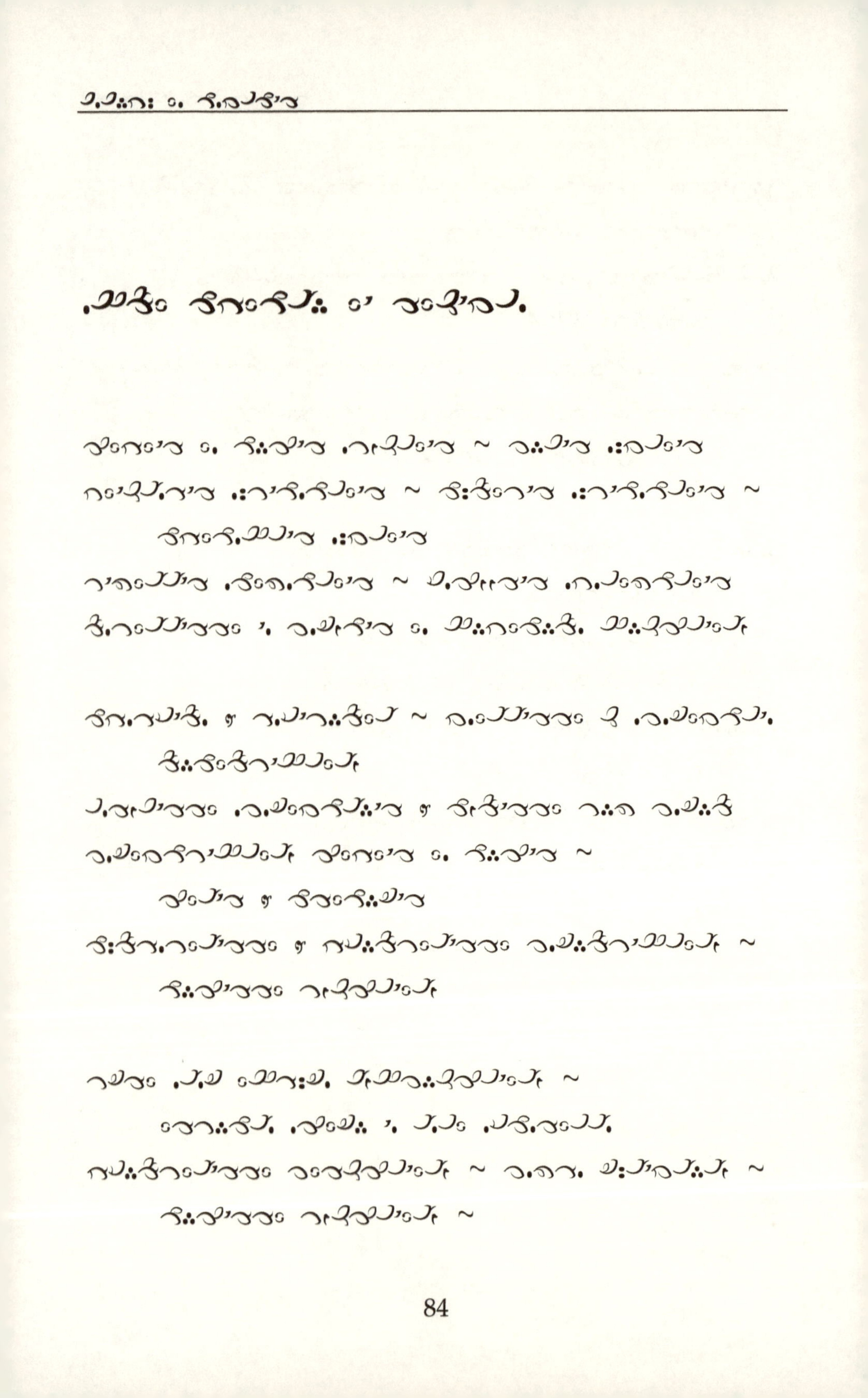

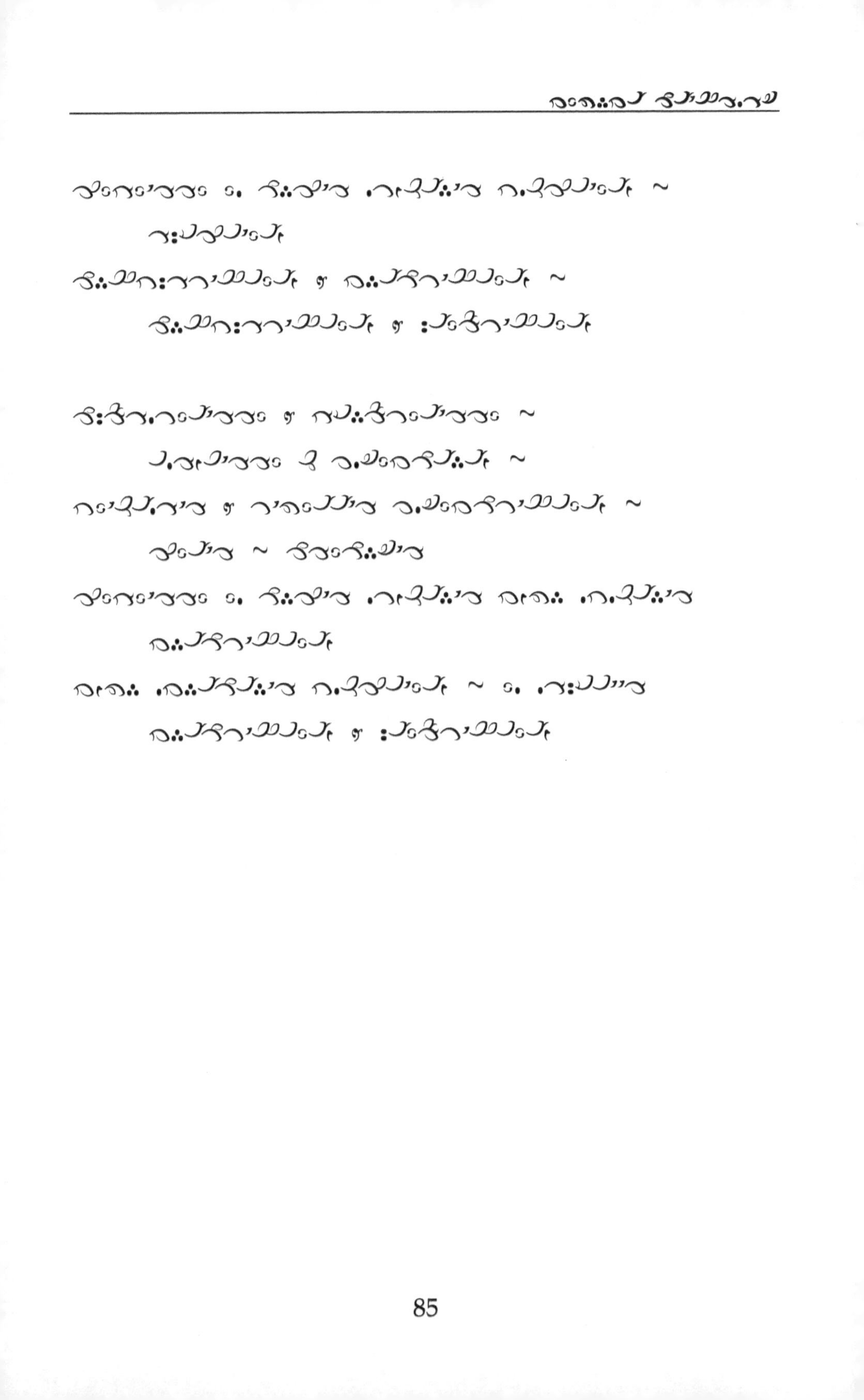

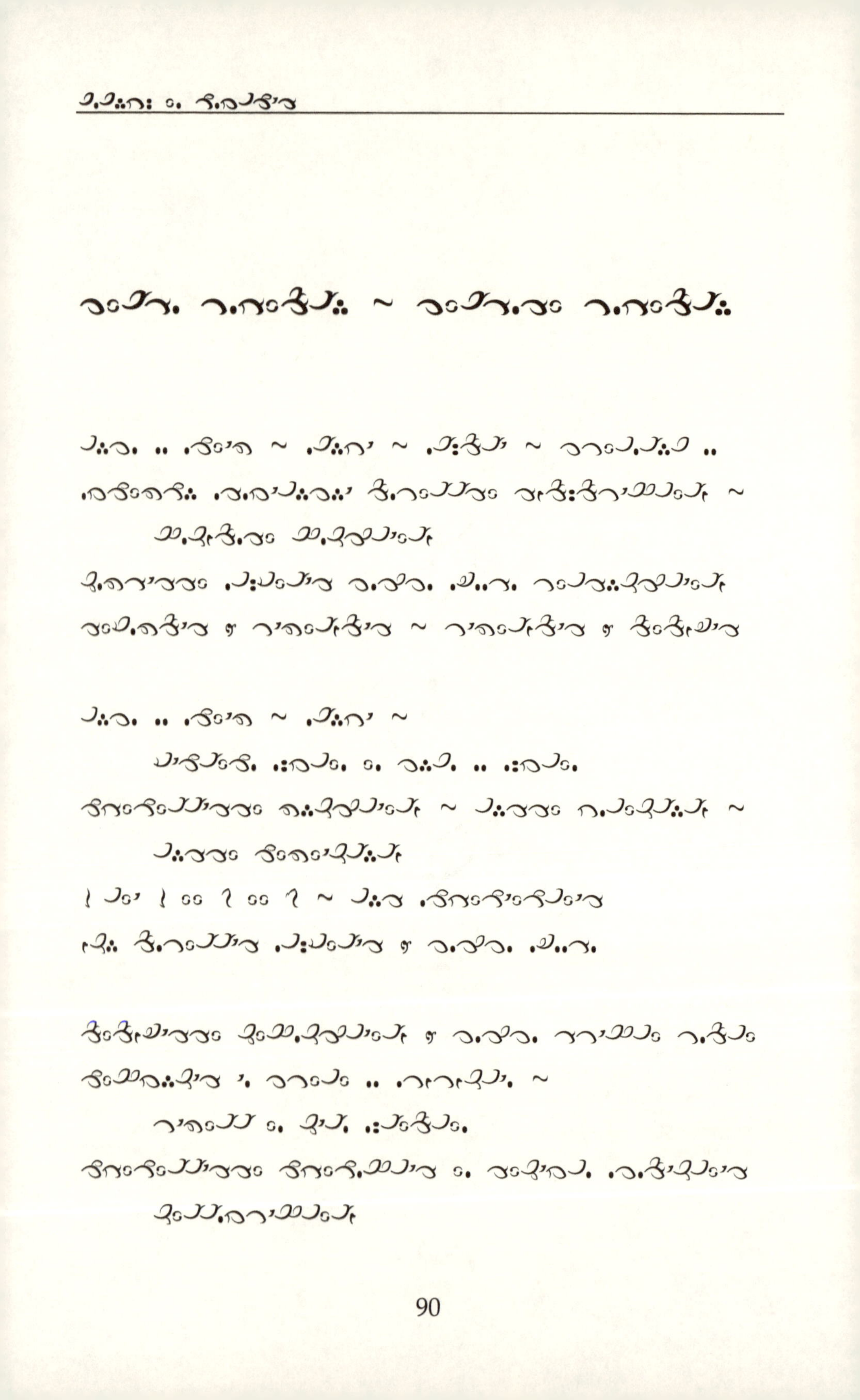

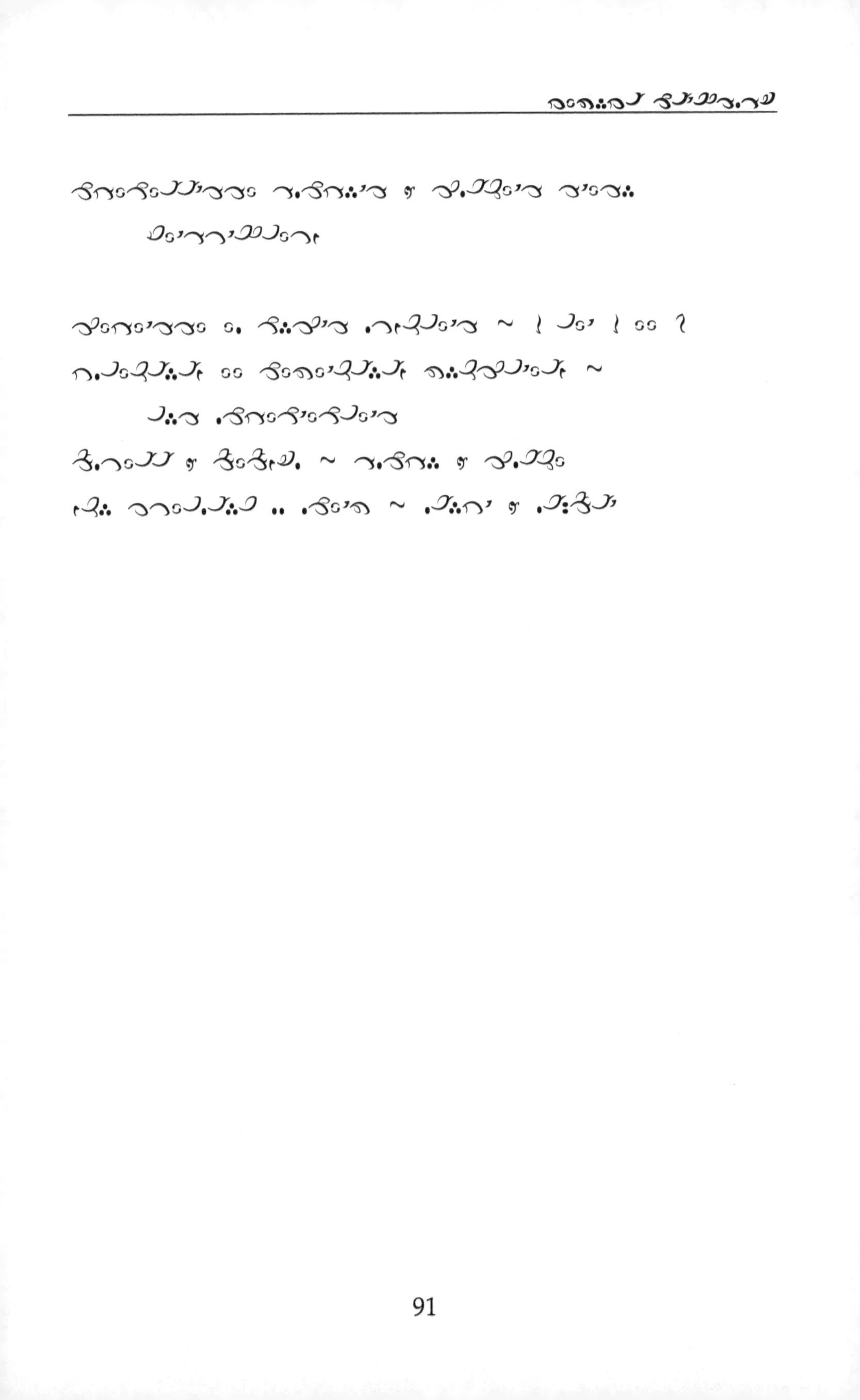

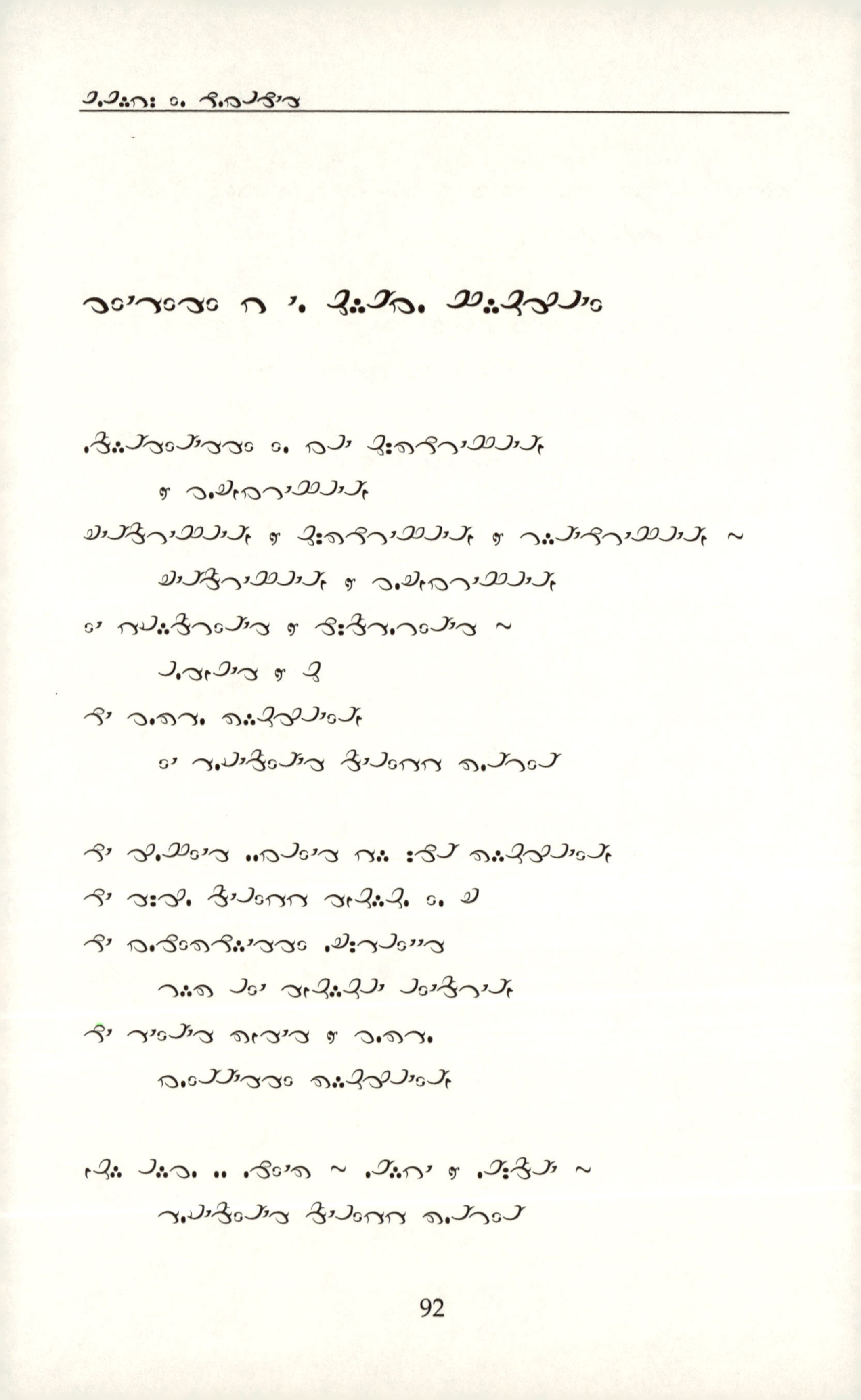

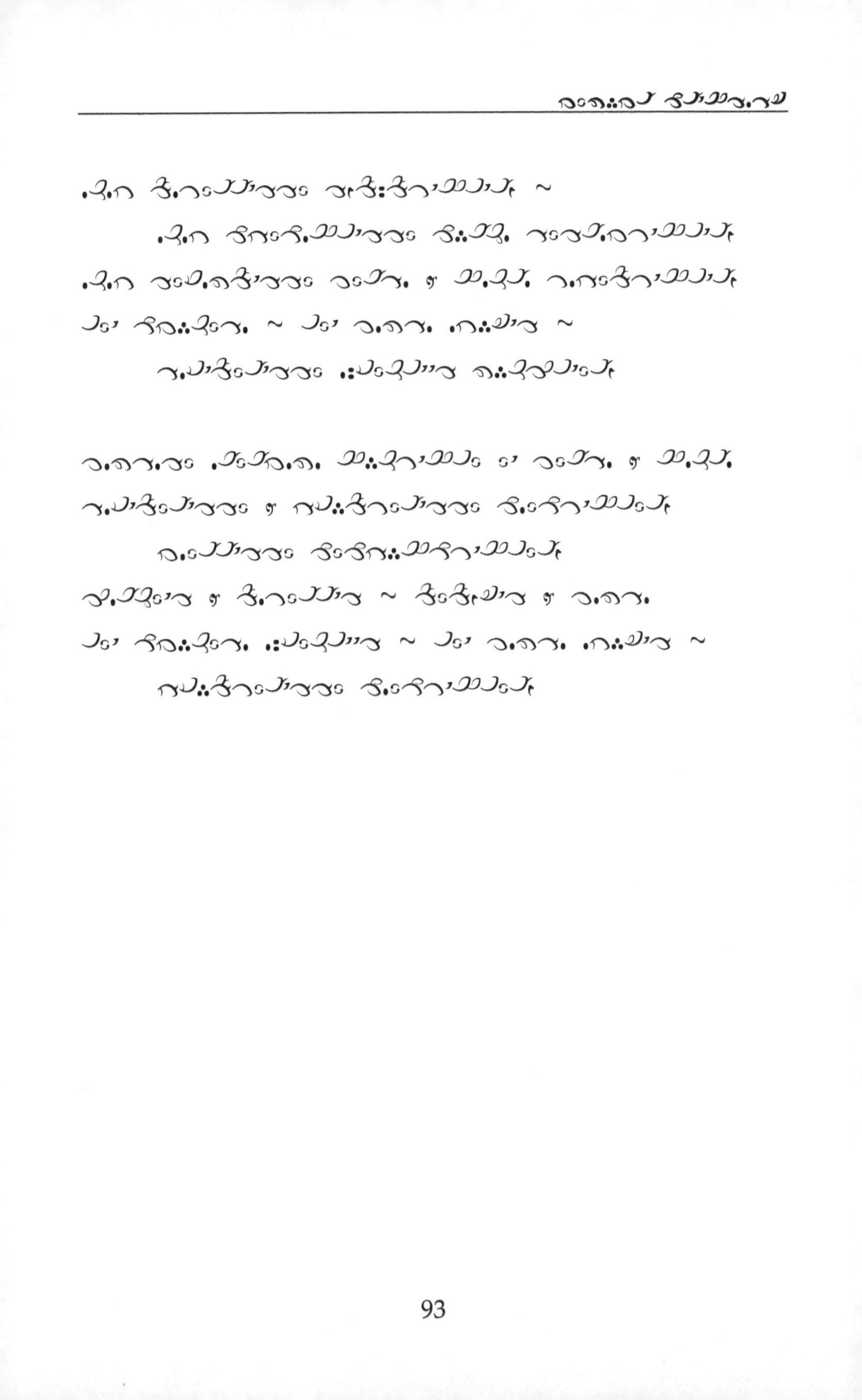

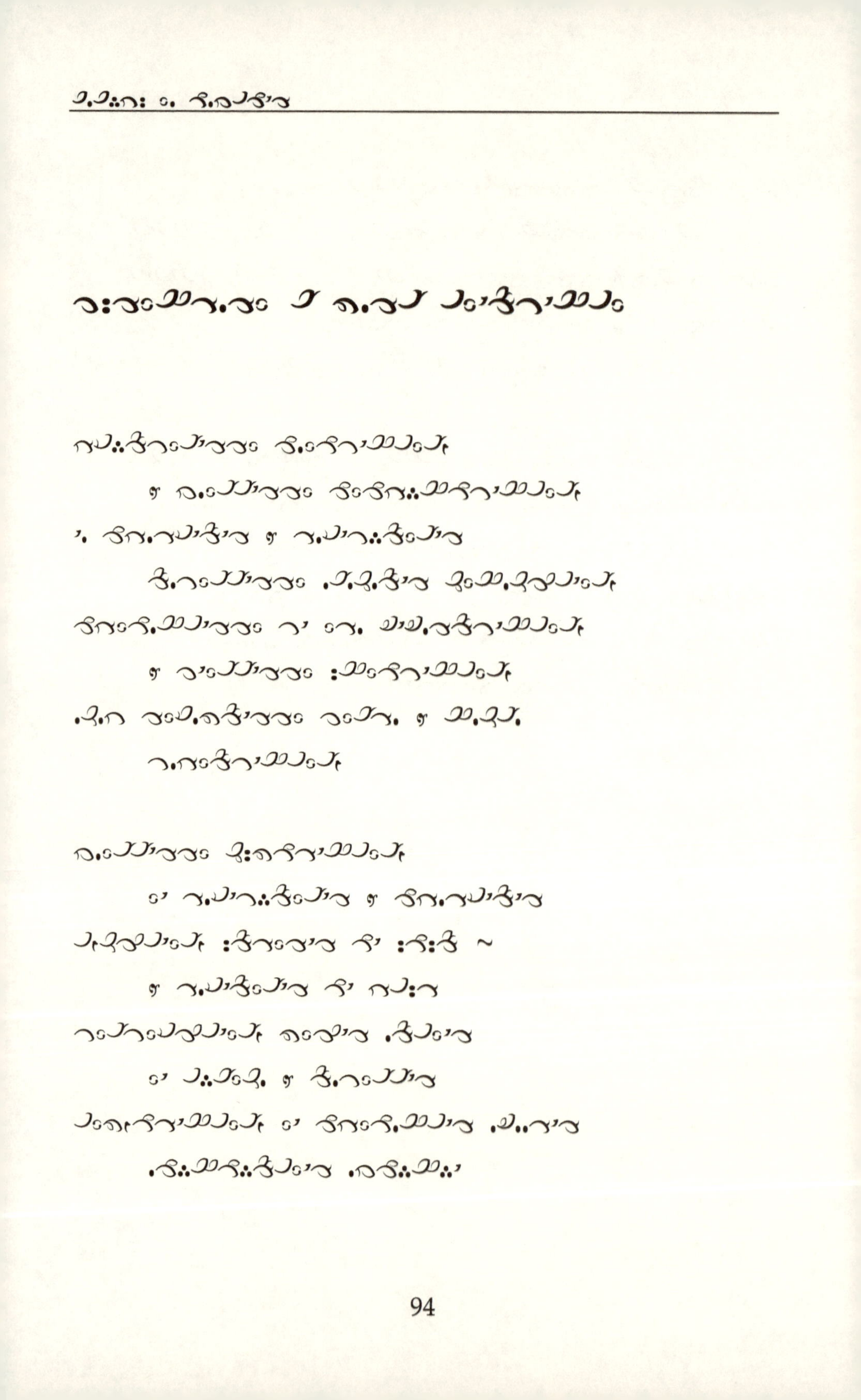

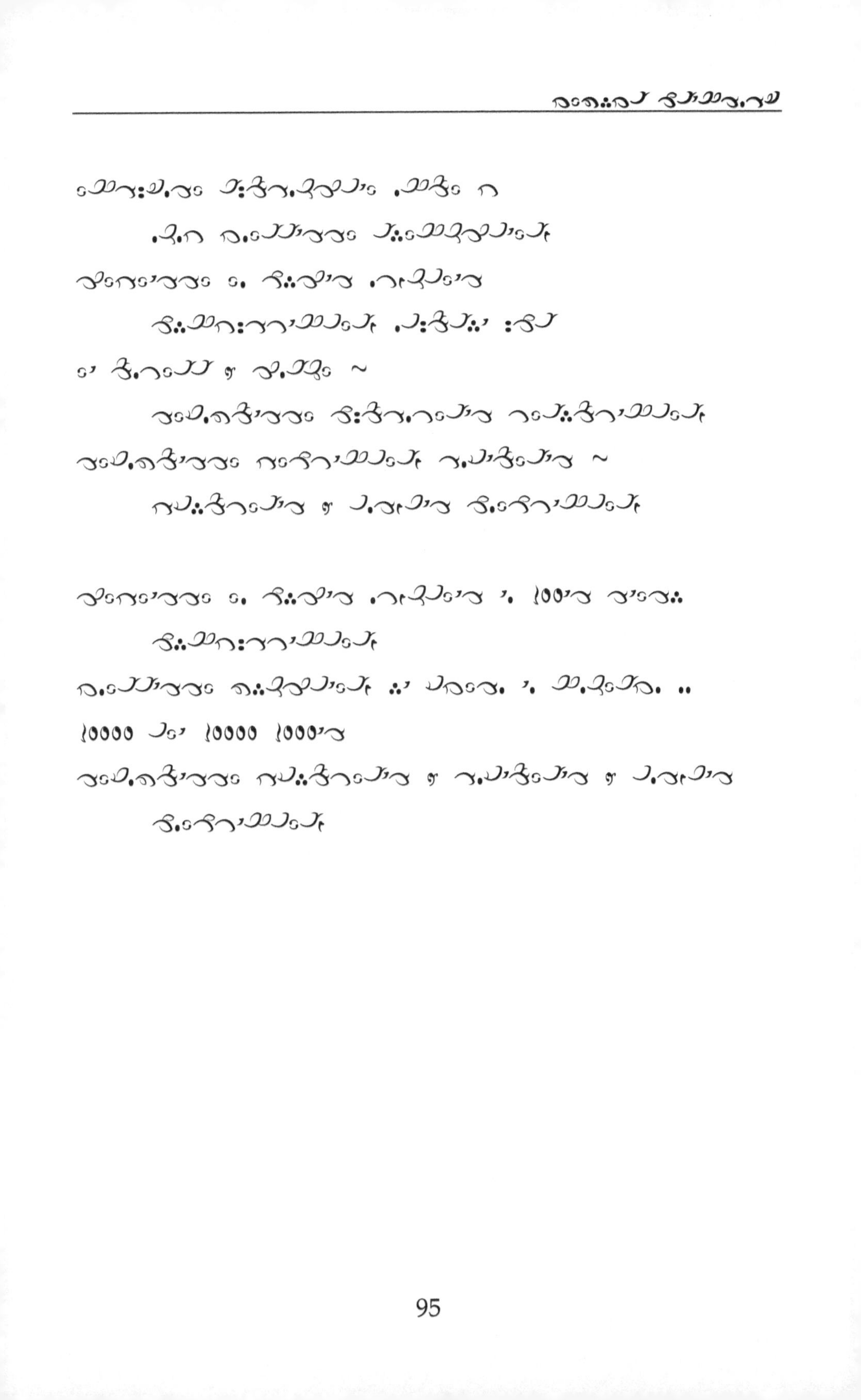

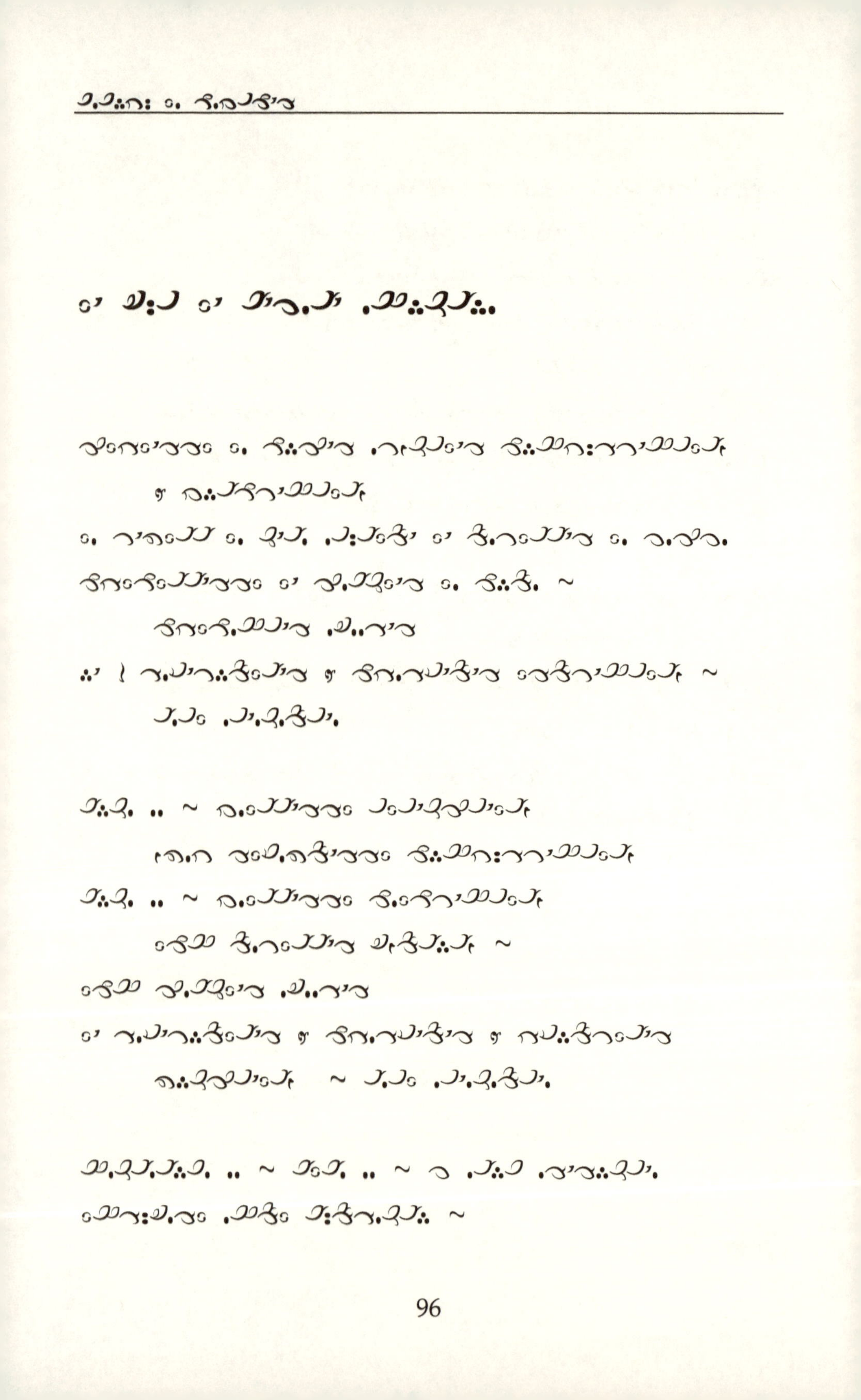

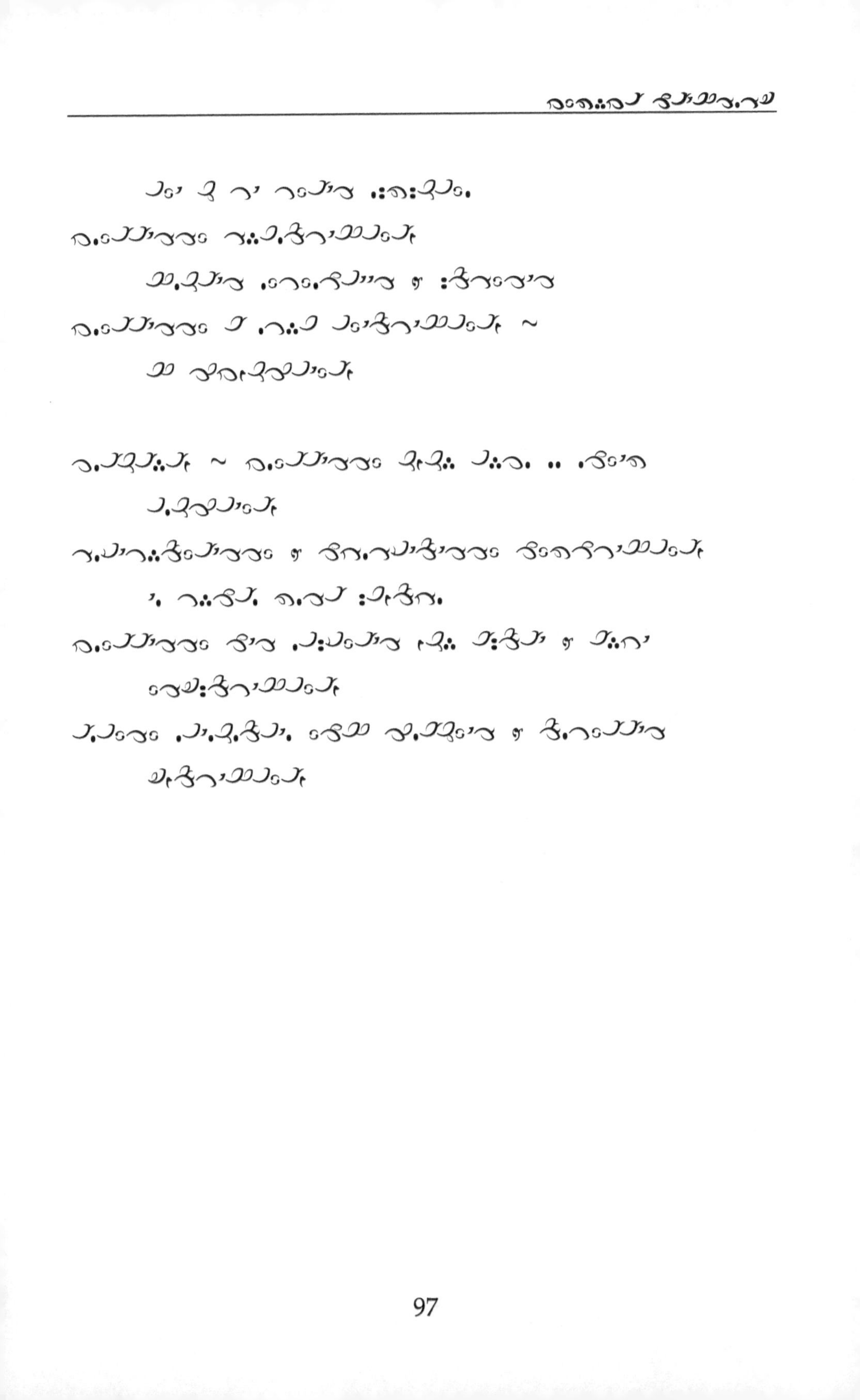

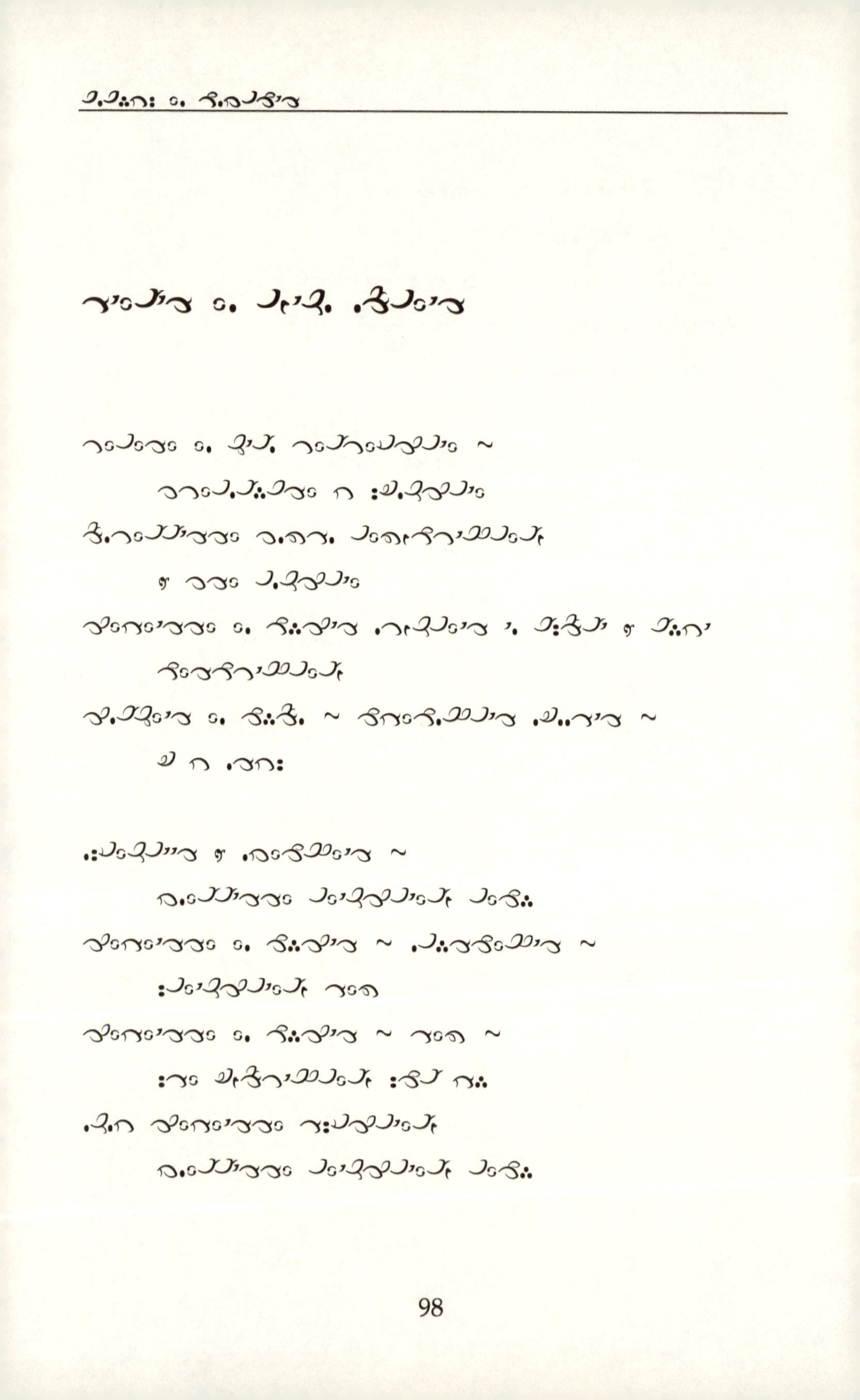

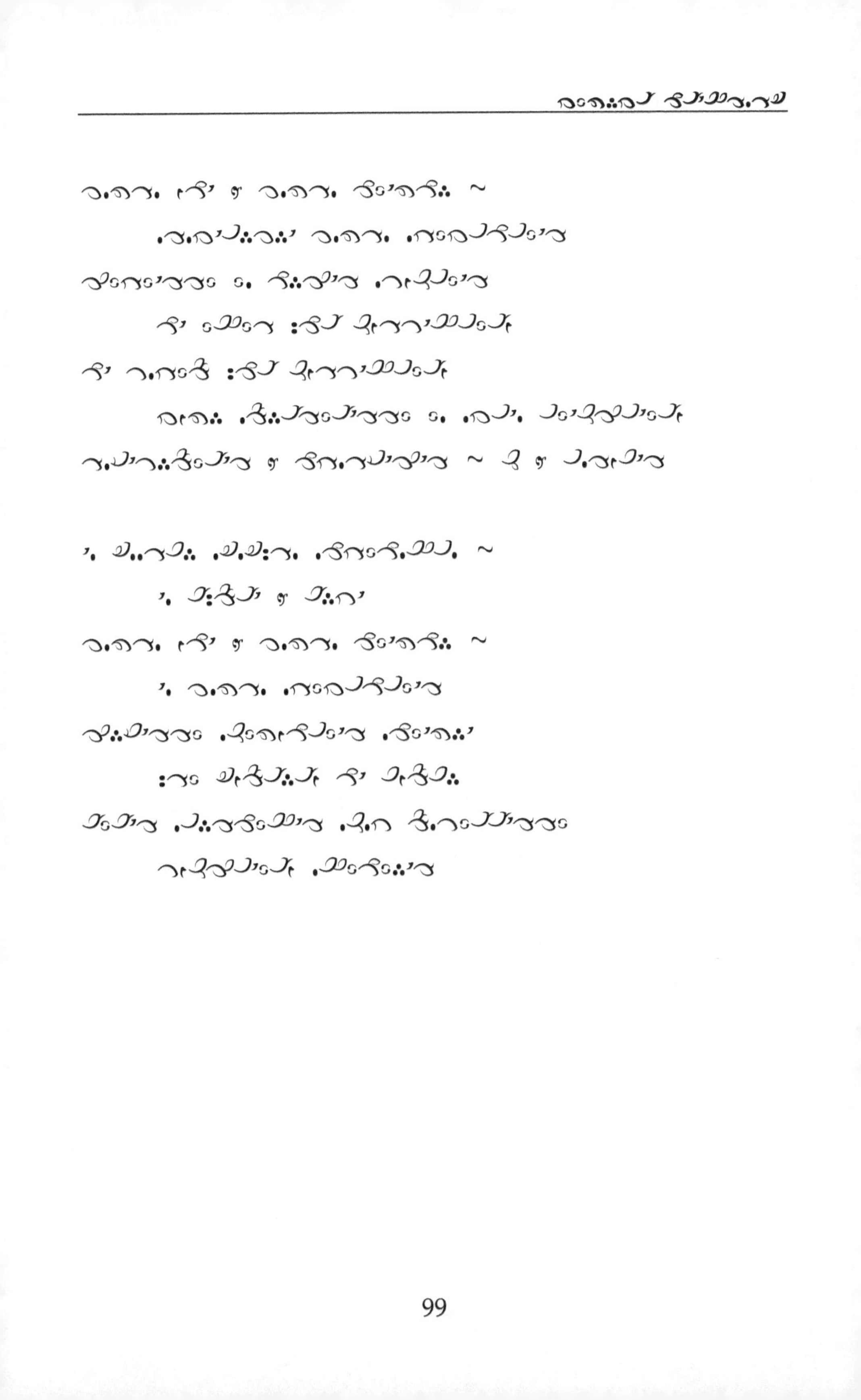

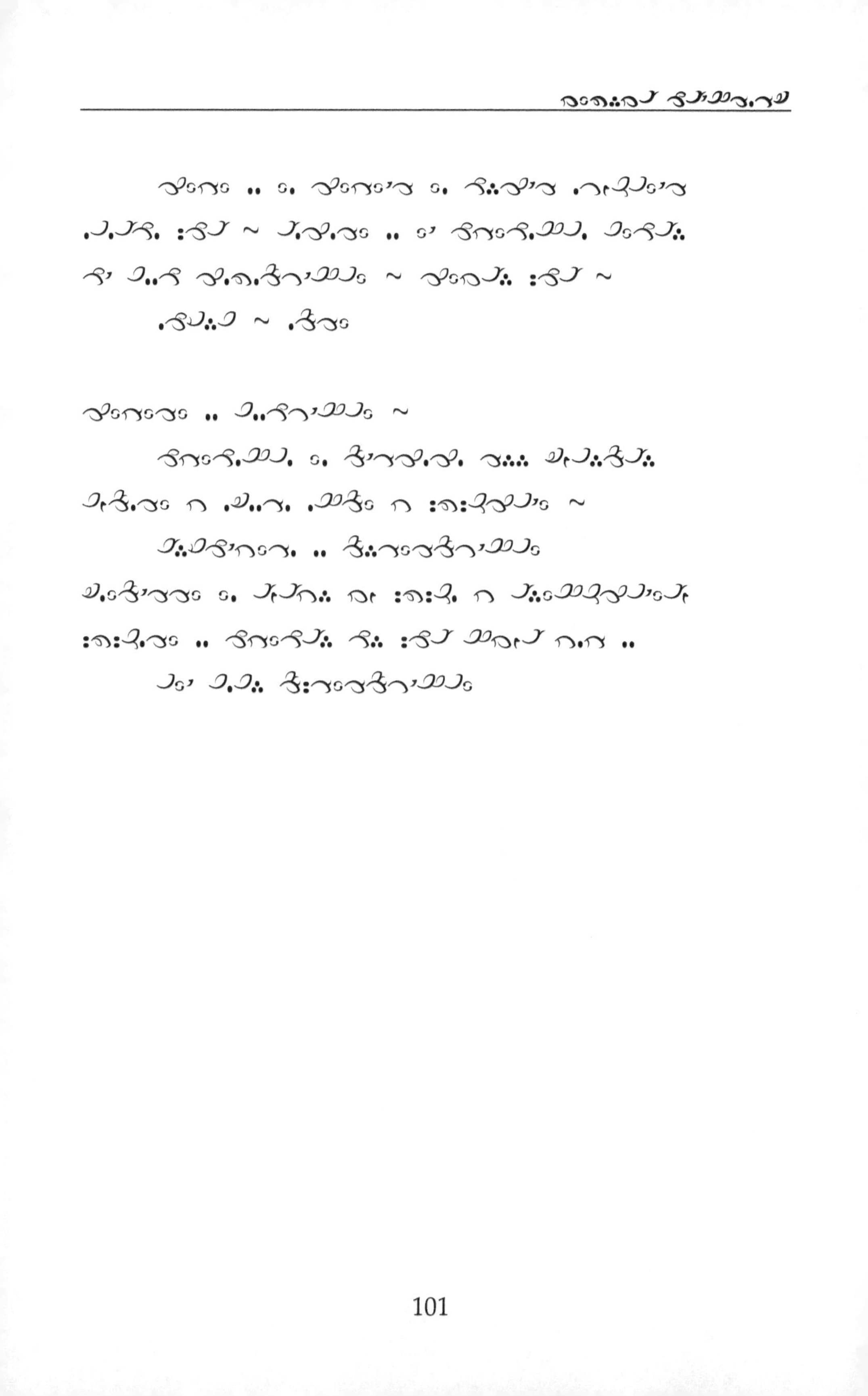

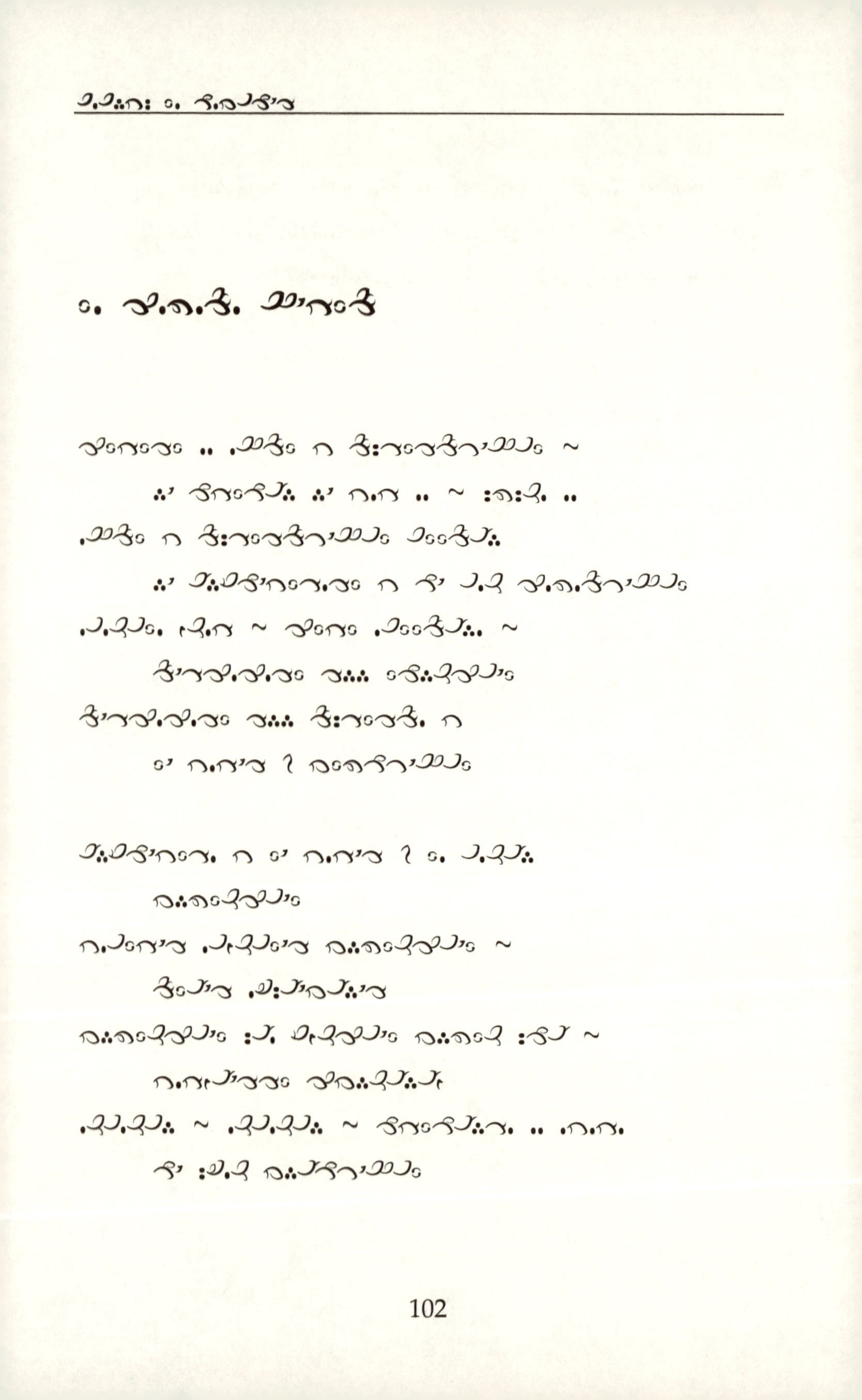

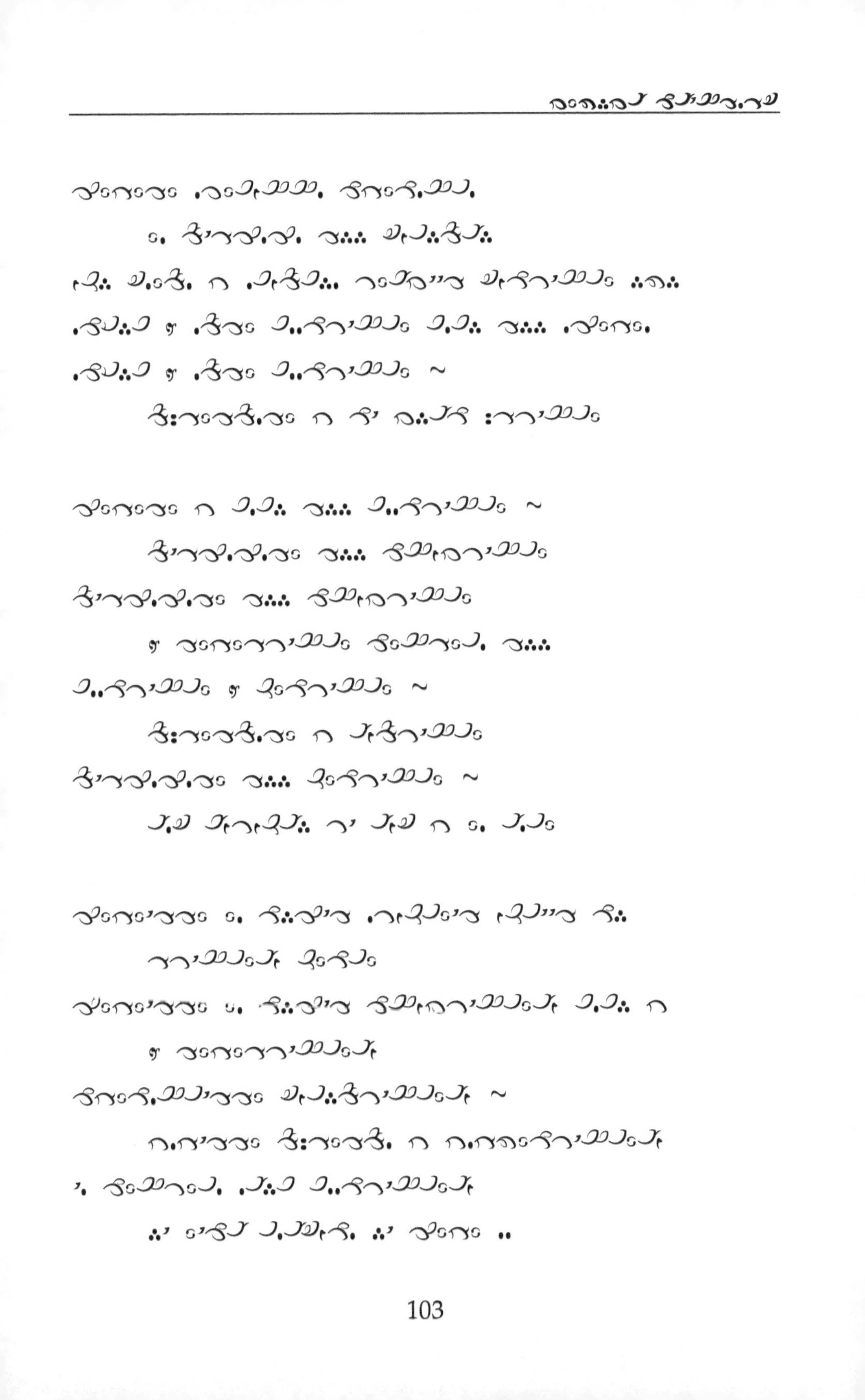

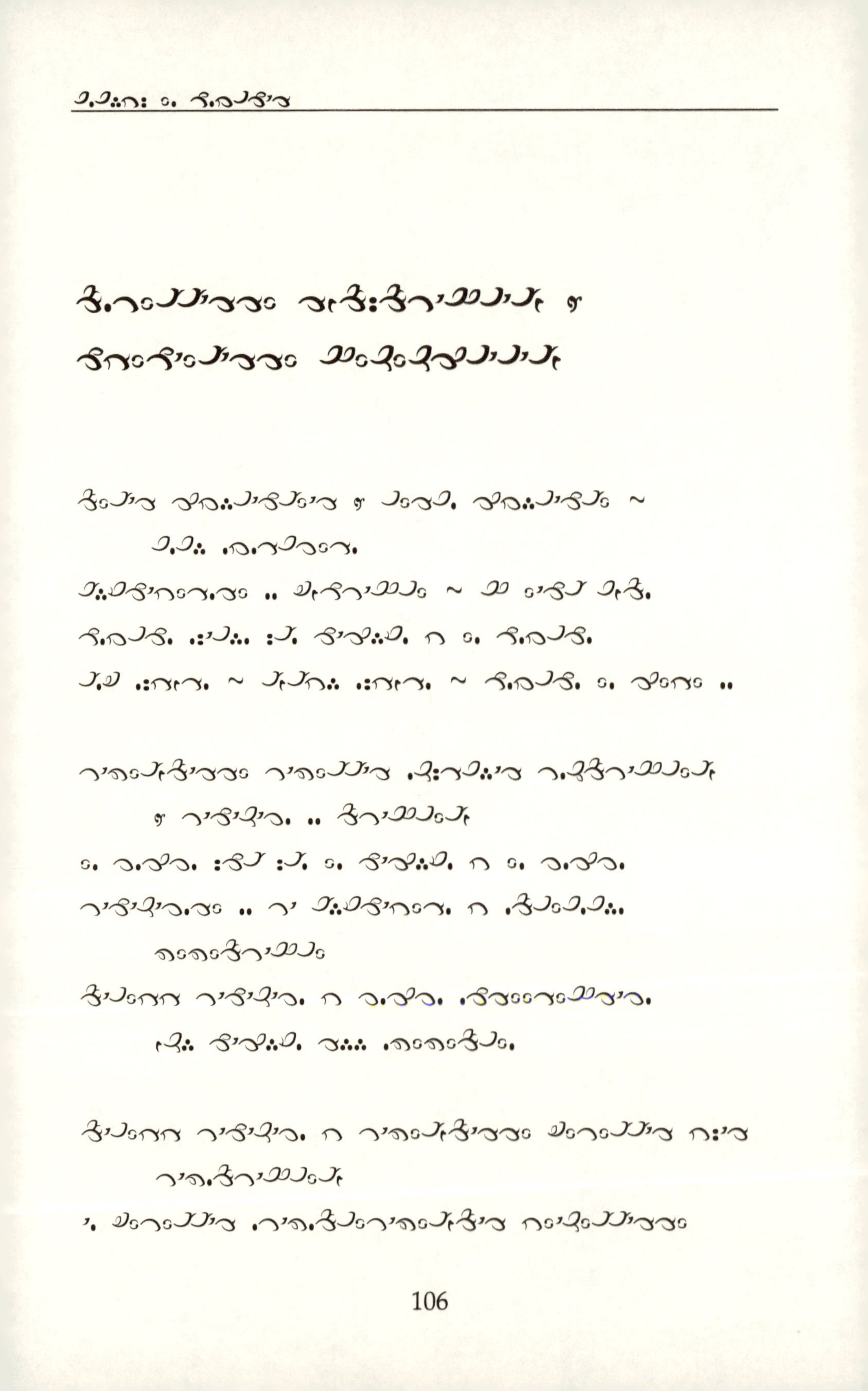

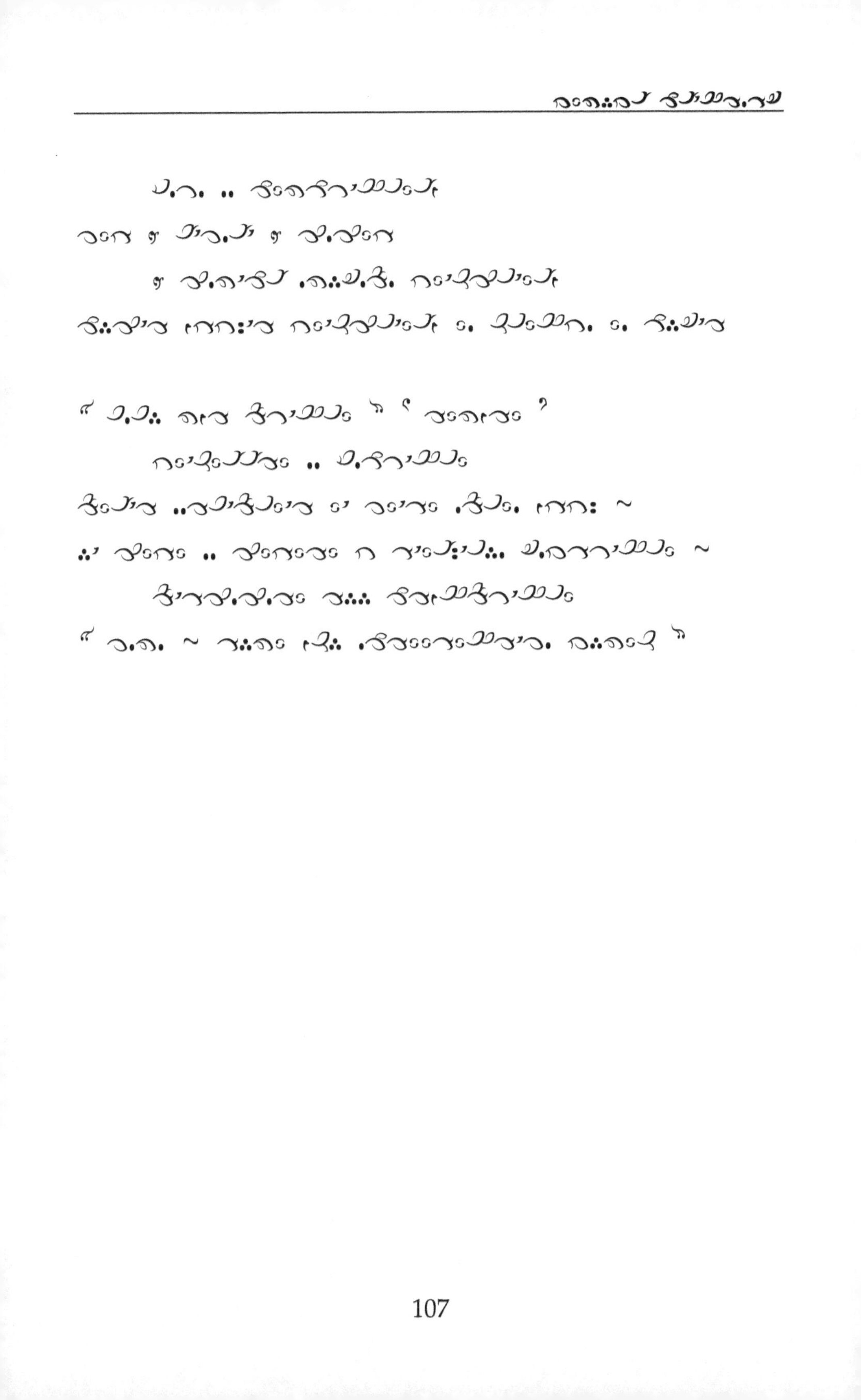

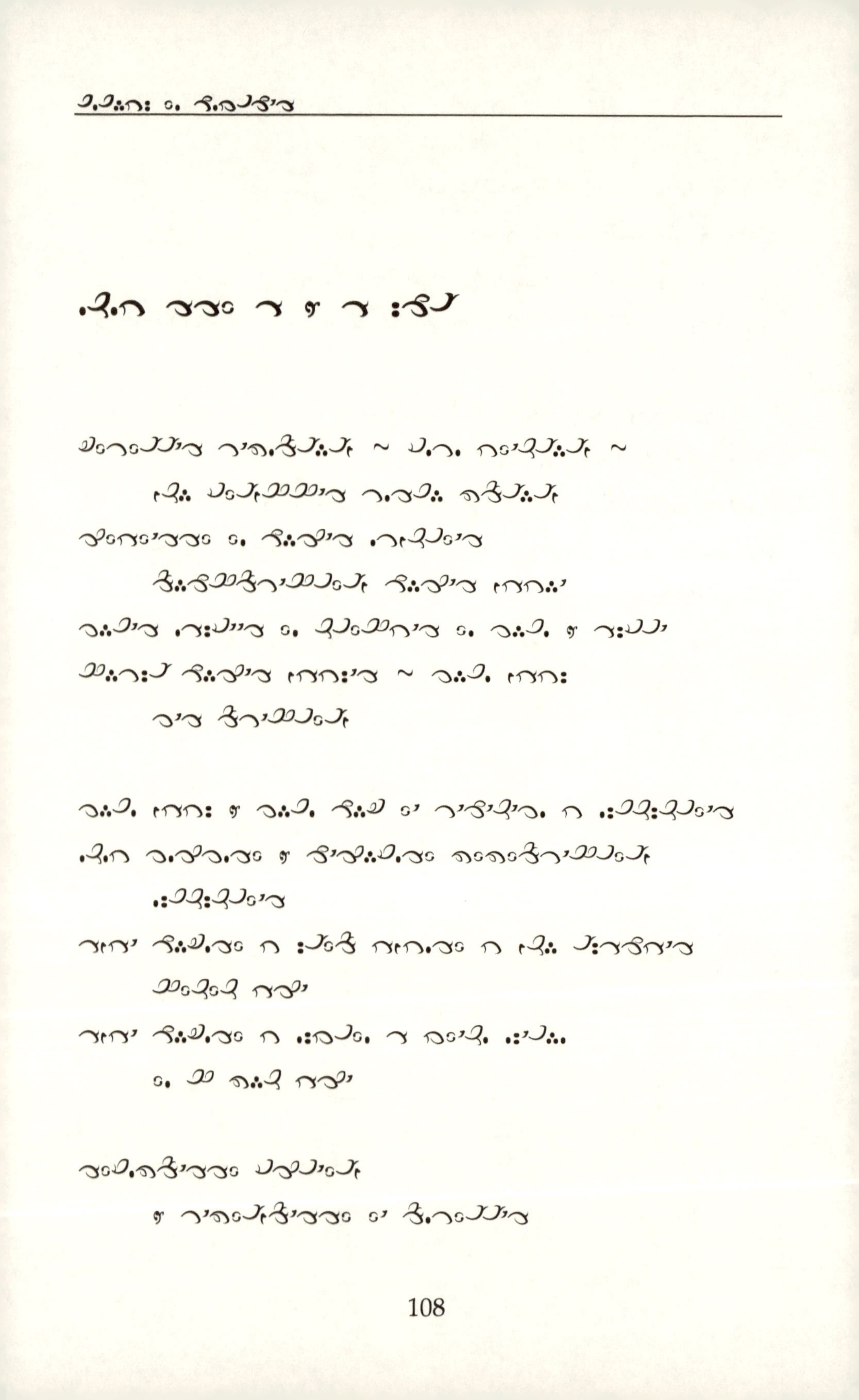

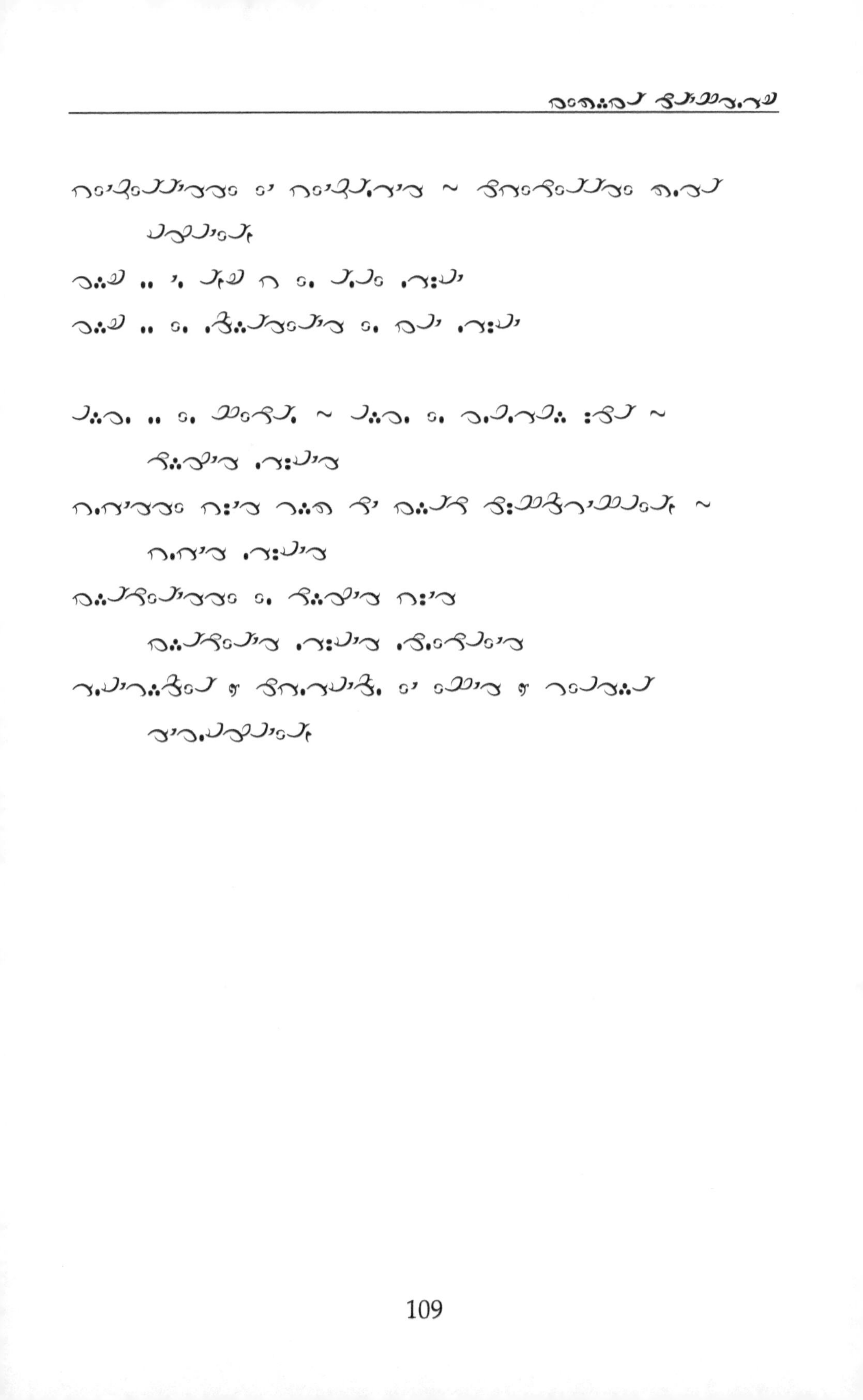

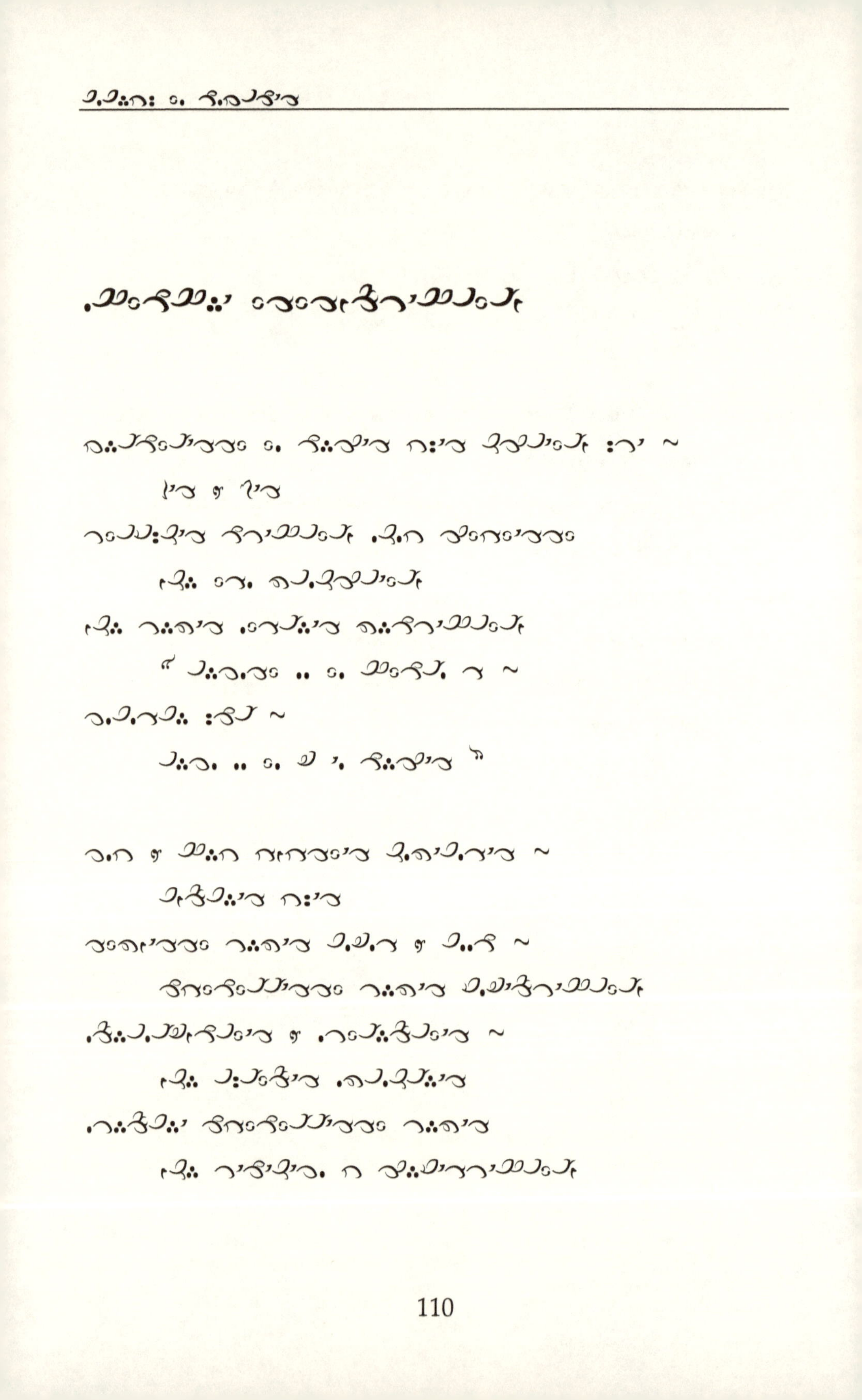

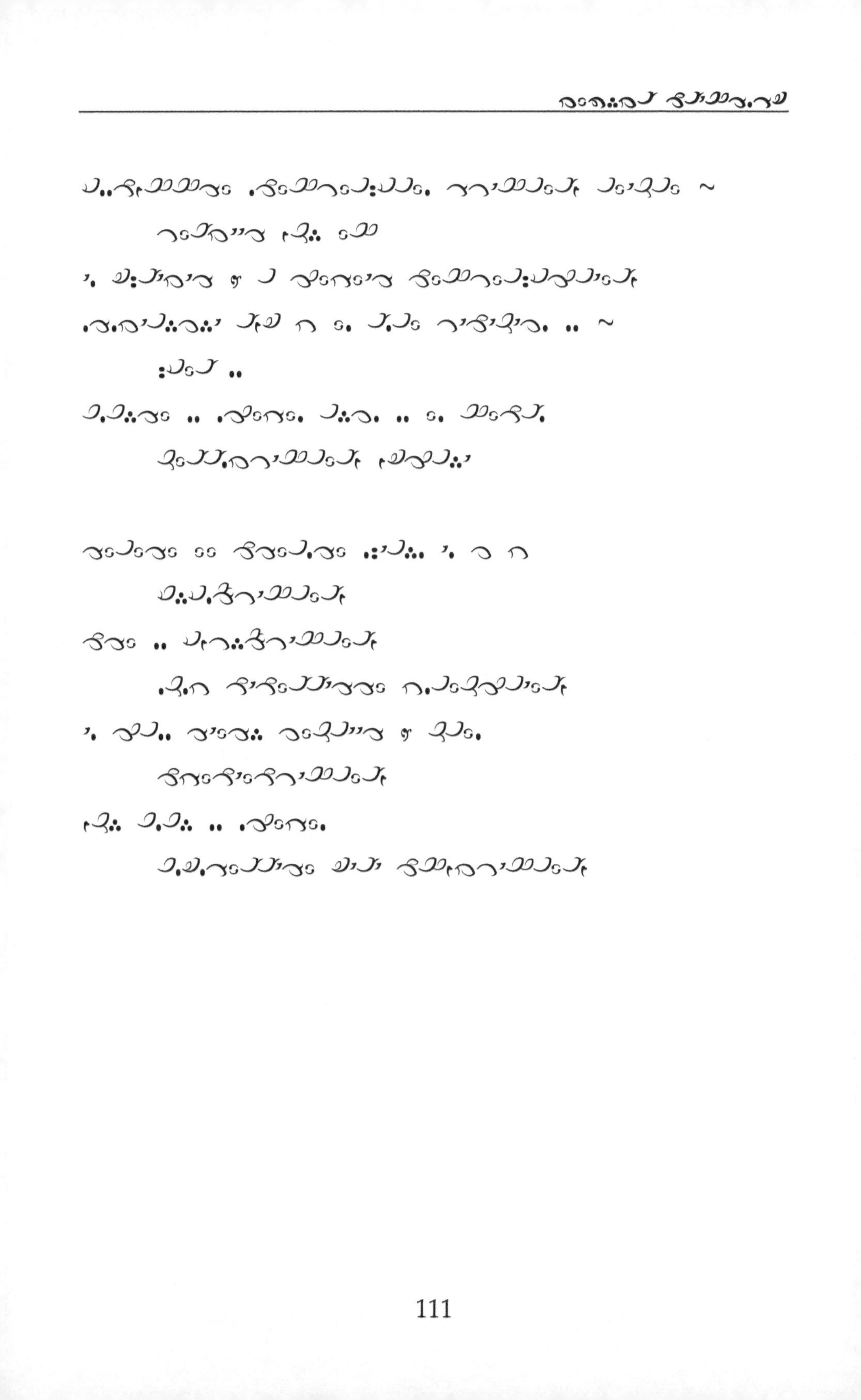

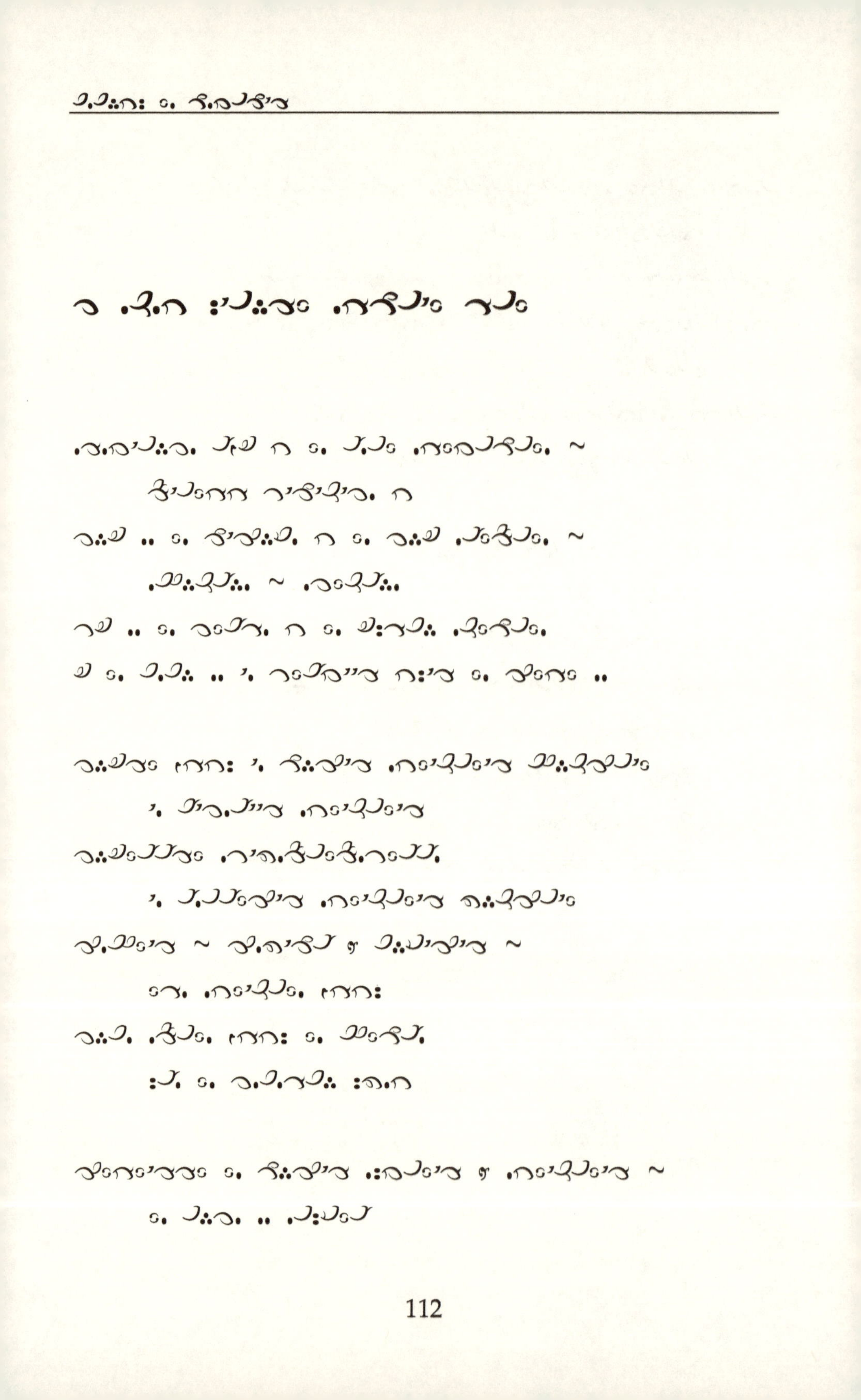

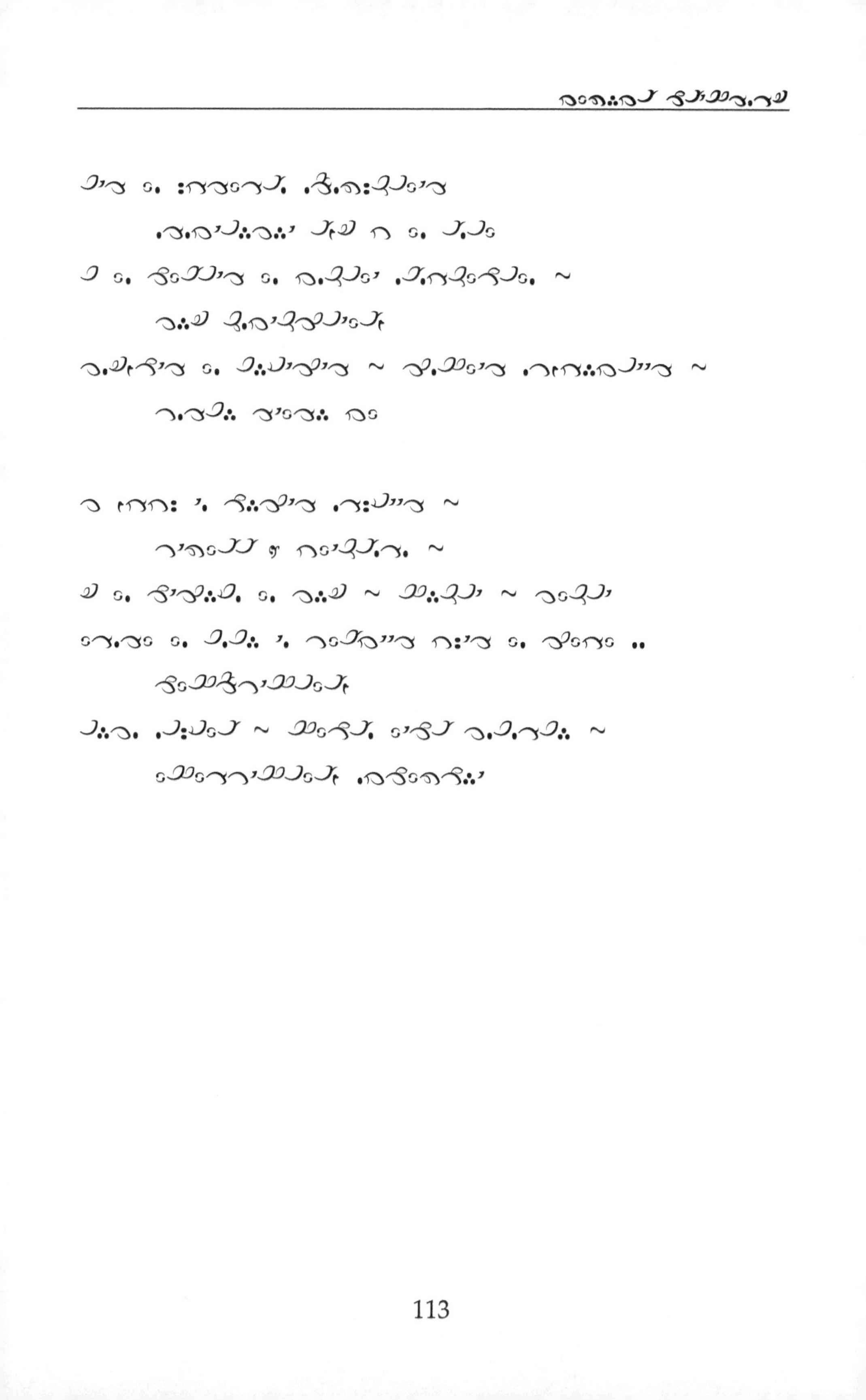

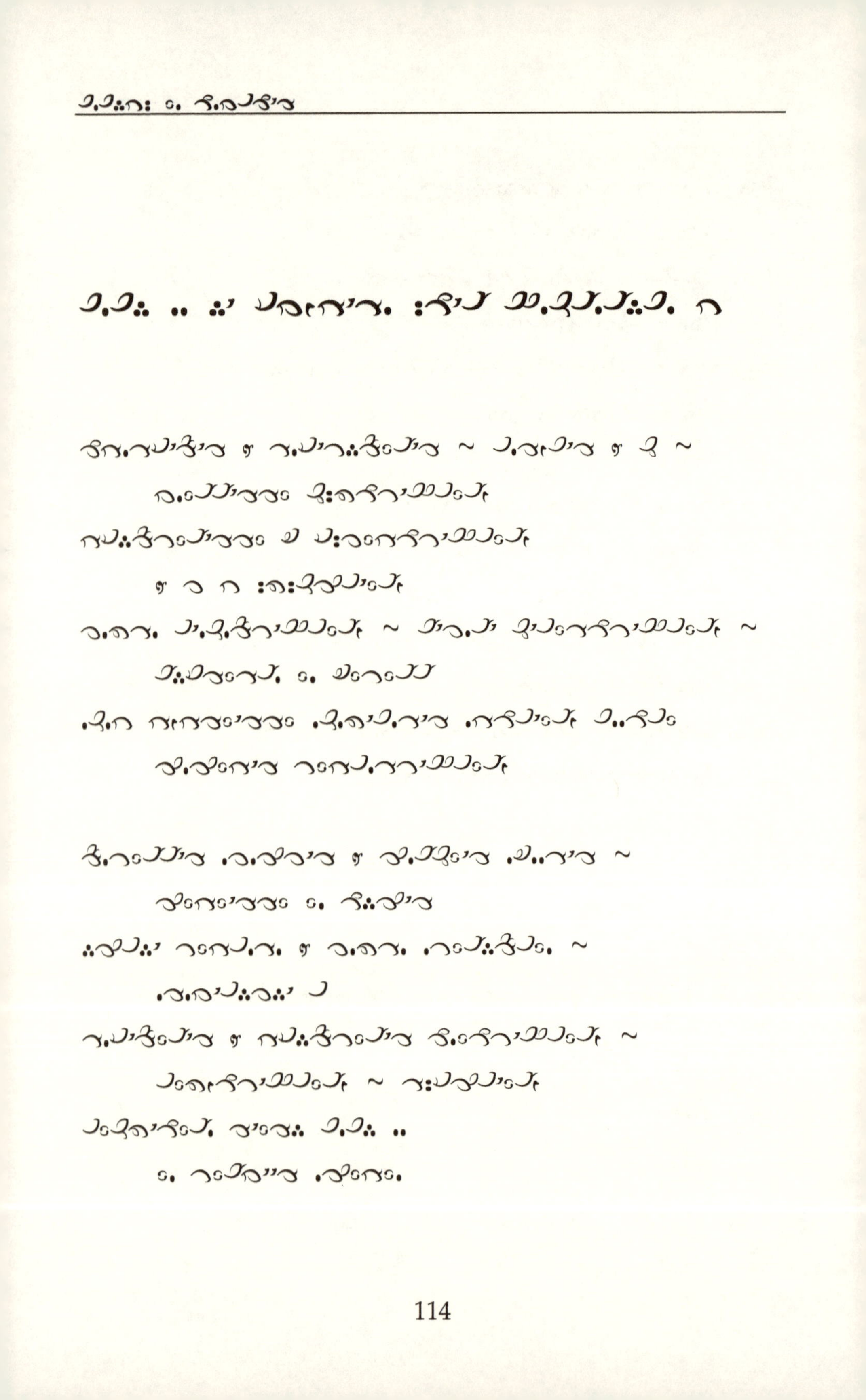

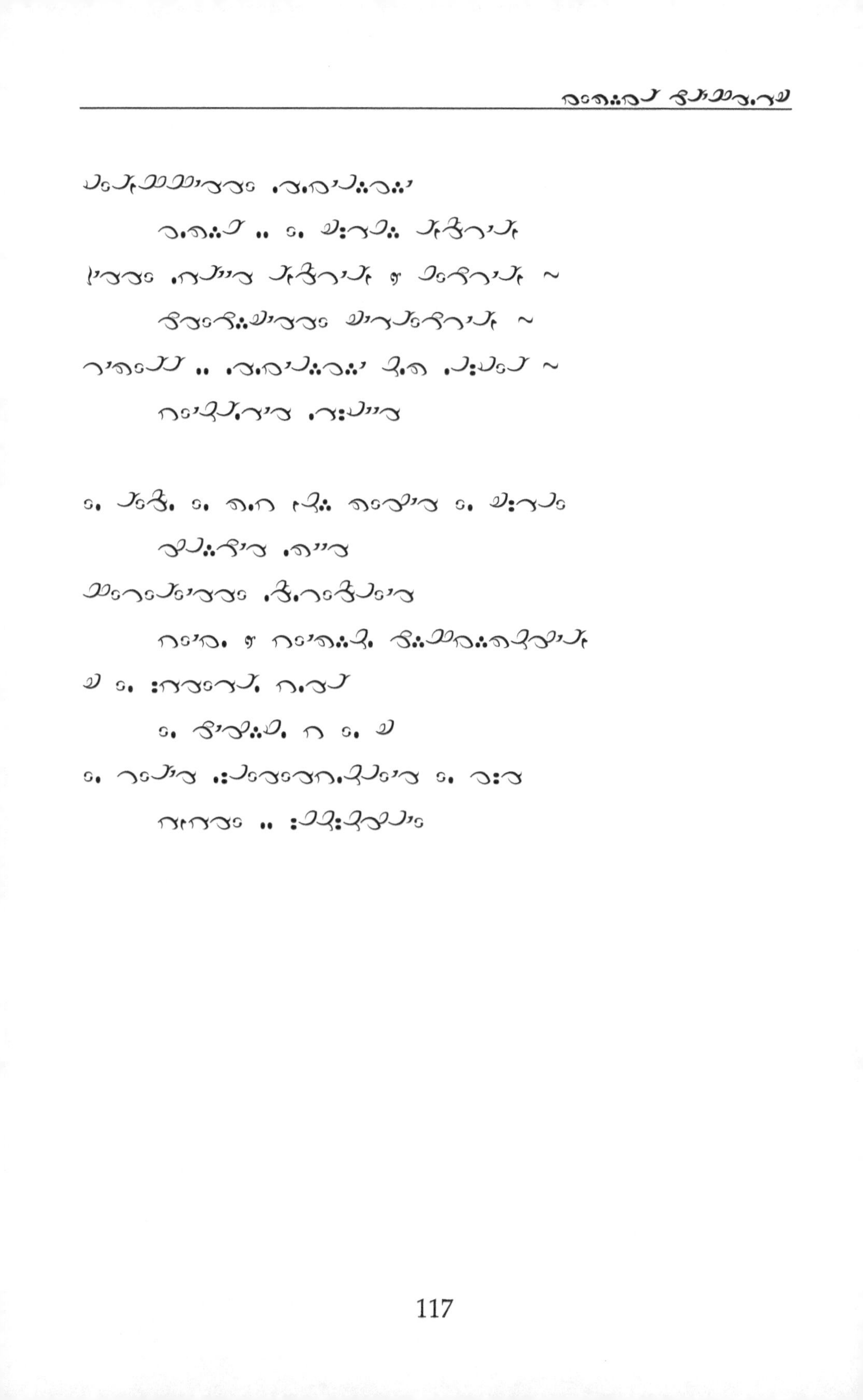

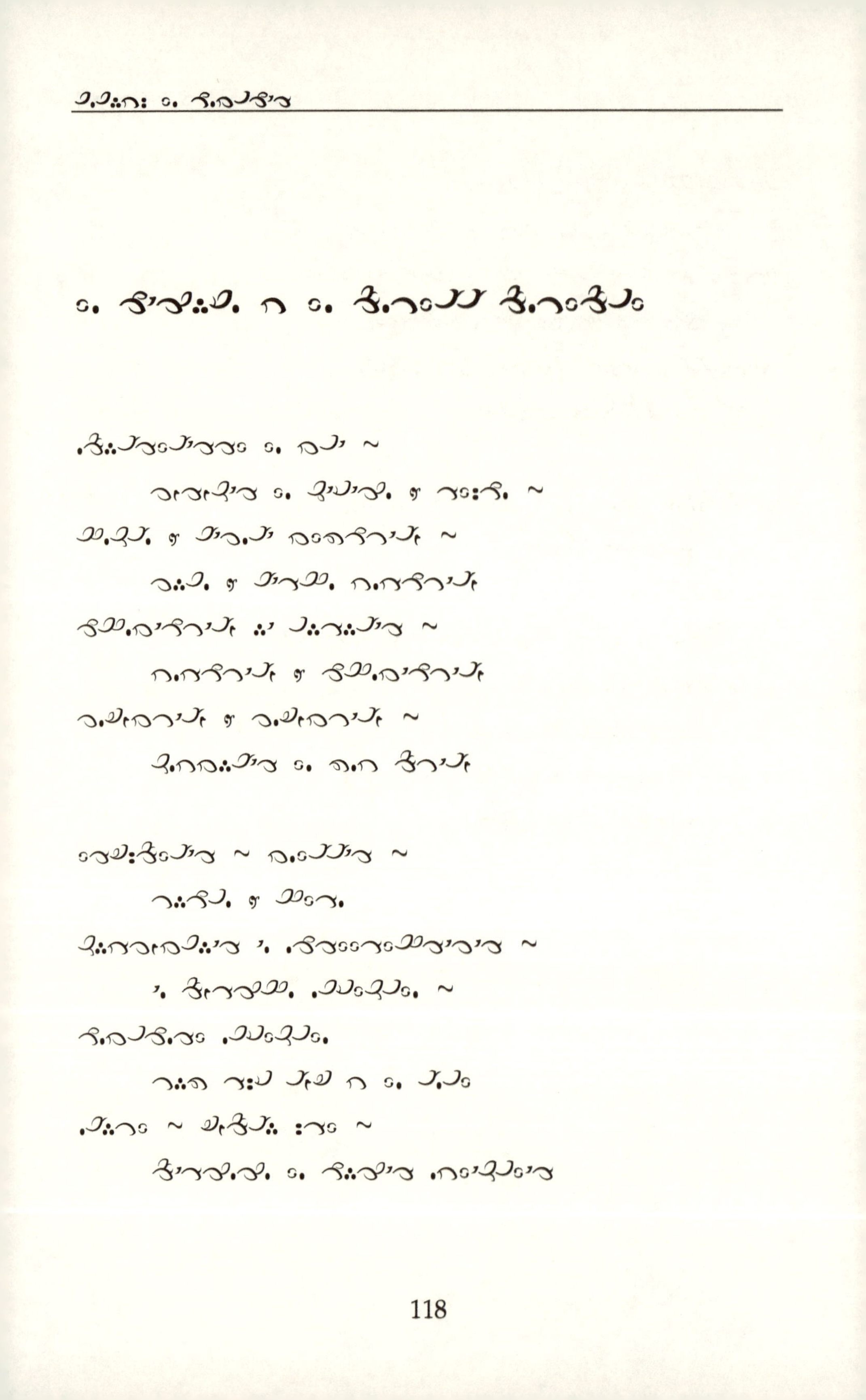

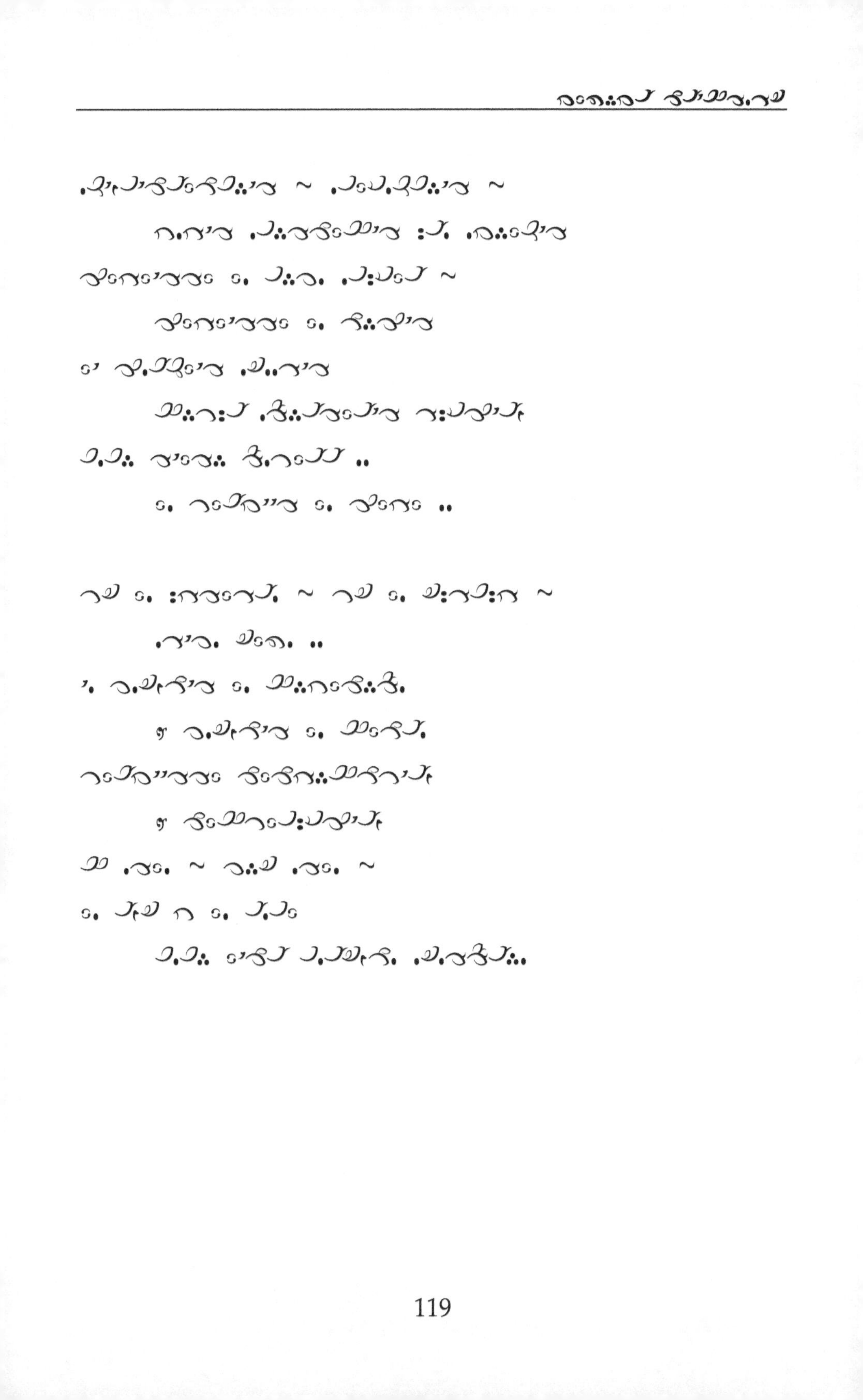

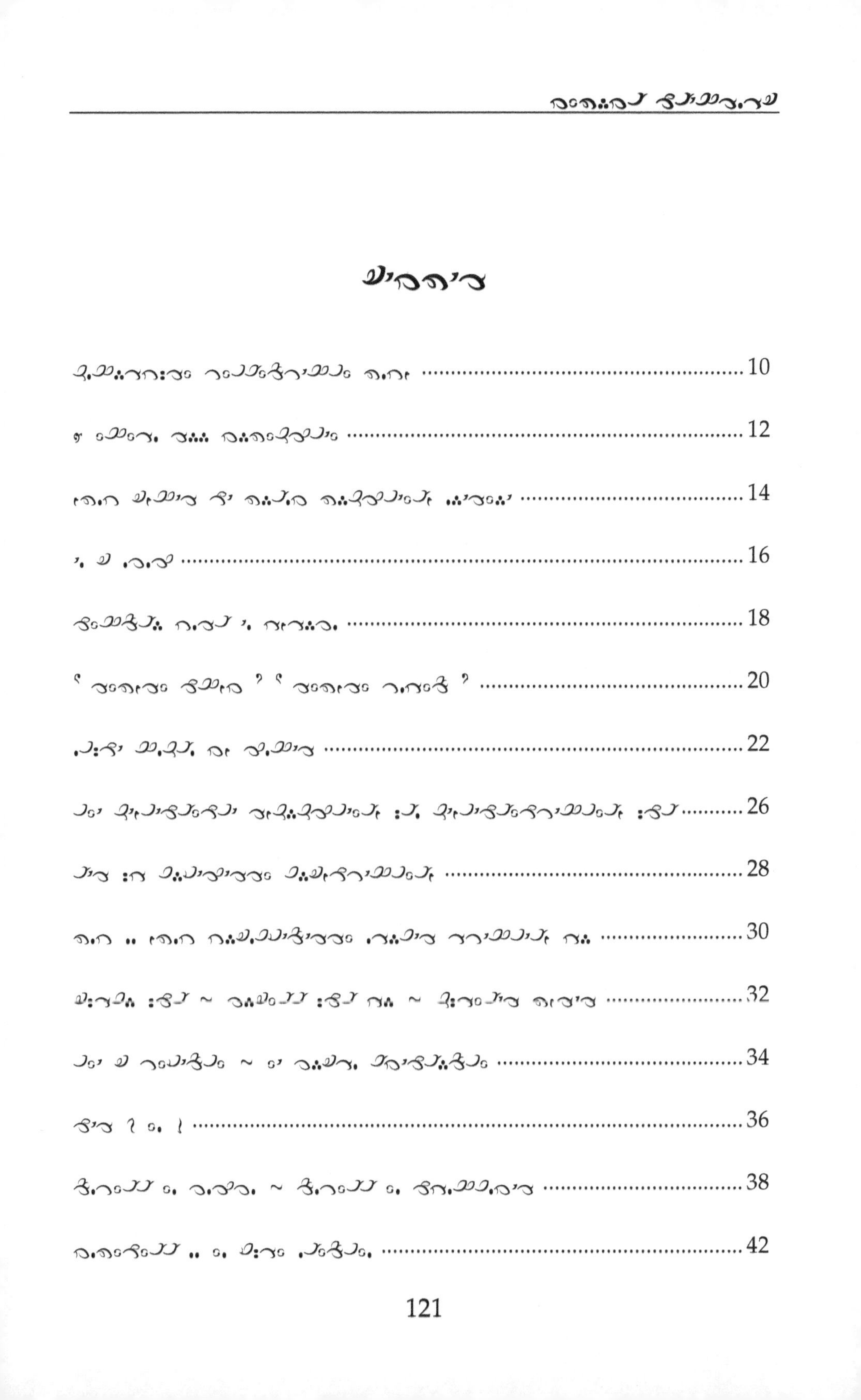

[illegible]

www.ingramcontent.com/pod-product-compliance
Lightning Source LLC
Chambersburg PA
CBHW030818200726
48288CB00004B/1280

* 9 7 8 1 7 3 2 1 1 8 7 0 6 *